Trail-Scarred

Will Petty's purchase of a provisioned trail wagon for the long trek west was his way of promising himself a quieter life, where a man might sit in the same shade more than once. The trek from the hills, however, raised a darkness not even the sharpshooting loner could match as a trio of bushwhackers rode in to rob, strip and leave him for dead in a bone-parched, dry-bed creek where the seasonal rains were not expected for weeks.

But then Will's luck changed in the shape of a travelling old-timer's prairie schooner and an agreement to a partnership that was to face the high stakes of a gold raid and leave only one gun seeking its personal retribution....

By the same author:

The Moonshiner
Bounty Gun
Gun Rage
Ocachi's Run
Killigan's Draw
Huckerman's Noon
Rogue Colt
Three Guns Waiting
The Jackson Raid

Trail-Scarred

LUTHER CHANCE

A Black Horse Western

ROBERT HALE · LONDON

ISBN 0 7090 7175 2

Robert Hale Limited
Clerkenwell House
Clerkenwell Green
London EC1R 0HT

KB 17.2.05

This one for T and Z, with fond wishes

Typeset by
Derek Doyle & Associates, Liverpool.
Printed and bound in Great Britain by
Antony Rowe Limited, Wiltshire.

ONE

He was a man with a silent past and a future he kept to himself. Will Petty came and went from the mountains to the mesa, the plains to the valleys as he saw fit and the mood took him. It was a way of life and had been for as long as he could recall.

He travelled light with few possessions save those he found necessary and the handful he prized. But that summer Will bought himself a wagon and team, stores, tools, wheat and flour, and headed West with the aim of settling a spread where a man might grow old peacefully and figure on enjoying the same shade more than once.

And so it was on a hot, cloudless day in July that he came to teasing and bouncing the wagon from the rutted hill range track to the gentler flats and fell to a steady pace for the town of Miriam.

Not until he was a half-mile down the trail and moving easy did he draw the spit-polished Winchester from its scabbard at his side and lay it across his knees in preparation for the trouble he knew was following.

*

The three riders had shadowed his progress since mid-morning, keeping to the narrow tracks high above him, always out of hailing range and never in full view for more than minutes at a time.

Drifters living rough and off their wits, Will had wondered; bushwhackers down on their luck and hoping for easy meat? Maybe they reckoned they had found it in one man driving a team and covered wagon through dry-bone country. All they had to do was watch and wait.

Will was of a patient, thoughtful nature, not given to hasty decisions or actions, who had learned through his long travelling life and the assorted types it had thrown across his path, to size a fellow carefully. What you saw at first glance was not always what you got; sometimes what you got you had never seen coming.

What he saw on that day drawing alongside him minutes later in a swirl of dust and snorting mounts looked as bad and unwelcome as he had ever seen.

The leading rider of the trio, already toting and waving a Colt as he snatched at the reins to the team to slow them, was a grisly-faced, broad-shouldered man with a brushing of black stubble, dark eyes and thick, fleshy lips.

The second rider drawn level with Will was a taller, thinner man with a bird-like expression, a beaky nose and bright pebble eyes. In addition to a holstered Colt, he also carried a furled bull whip that looked as if it never left his hand.

The third man, bucking and bouncing his mount and whooping excitedly through a thin, piping voice, was altogether the 'kid' of the party; younger, fair-haired and fresh-faced, with chillingly sharp blue eyes that seemed pressed into their shallow sockets like crystals.

'Whoa there. Whoa,' called Will, reining back heavily as the team slithered to a dusty halt and the wagon creaked and groaned in protest.

The Colt-toting rider came forward slowly to face Will, his mount snaffling at the pestering flies. 'You bound for Miriam, mister?' he growled, his teeth grating on trail dirt.

'I figured so,' said Will quietly.

'Sodbuster,' tittered the younger man. 'I see a sodbuster here. Got it scrawled all over him. That what you are, mister, a sodbuster?'

Will shrugged dismissively. 'No, wouldn't say that. Nothin' like.'

The man with the bull whip spat across the dirt. 'Packed wagon here. Most of it fresh.' He spat again. 'Where yuh from? Where yuh headin'?'

'No business of yours, way I see it.' Will's eyes narrowed.

'Lip-smart with it,' cackled the kid. 'A lip-smart sodbuster would yuh know?'

'What's your business in Miriam?' growled grisly-face again.

Will took his time before he answered. 'Passin' through.'

'So he ain't expected,' grinned bull whip. 'So he won't be missed. Ain't this our lucky day?'

Will's fingers closed carefully in his grip on the Winchester.

Grisly-face levelled his Colt. 'Throw down the rifle, mister, then you step down yourself. Real slow. Real quiet.'

Will hesitated, his gaze moving slowly over the faces of

the men watching him. Three to one, he mused; he would take out one, maybe wing a second, but the third would get him, plumb as a stone to a pond, and that would be that.

But if he threw the rifle down and stepped to it as close as he dared. . . .

The rifle hit the dirt and Will came slowly after it, careful to keep his back to the wagon.

'That's better,' smiled bull whip. 'Now we can get to seein' what you're carryin' back there.'

'Stores, wheat, flour, linen . . . nothin' of note,' murmured Will, anxious to hold the attention away from the rifle.

'See, it's like I said,' cackled the kid. 'He's a sodbuster. Only sodbusters carry that sort of trash.'

'That sort of trash, as you put it, baby-face, fetches a good price among travellers,' clipped bull whip. 'And this outfit ain't in that bad shape neither. I reckon —'

'T'ain't for sale,' snapped Will. 'Nothin's for sale.'

The kid tittered and dribbled saliva over his chin. Grisly-face twisted his shoulders, releasing the cloying stench of old sweat on an unwashed body. Bull whip simply smiled. 'Who said anythin' about buyin'?' he asked, raising his sand-streaked eyebrows.

'We sure as hell never did,' grinned the kid, tipping his hat from his brow. 'Fact, I don't recall ever buyin' anythin', leastways not lately.'

Will's gaze tightened. He was closing fast on a state of crisis here, he thought, licking his lips.

'No, we ain't buyin', mister,' gestured bull whip. 'And if you ain't sellin' . . . why, I do declare looks to me as if we're about to be takin'.' He rolled the furled whip through his grip. 'How's that suit yuh, mister? You all for seein' this out along them terms, or are we goin' to get to arguin' this in detail? We ain't in no hurry.'

Will stiffened, his glance darting quickly to the Winchester at his boot. Could he grab it, level it, fire it before one of the three reacted? Would he have the time?

Grisly-face rolled his shoulders again. 'It's gettin' hot. What say we finish this and get ourselves through to town? Fancy myself one of them gals back there at the Dollar Bit.'

'I'm for that,' said the kid, slapping his thigh. 'But let's do this like we always do, eh? Have ourselves some laughs. Hell's fire, it's only a loose-lipped sodbuster we got here.'

Bull whip slid slowly, carefully from his mount, his beaky nose seeming to sharpen, his pebble eyes to gleam. 'Sure we will,' he grinned, sweat beginning to glisten on his cheeks. 'Sure . . . let's have ourselves some real big laughs!'

And then the bull whip cracked.

TWO

Will fell to the first lash, his legs dragged from under him as the whip curled round his ankles and threw him to the dirt. He scrambled wildly for the cover of the wagon, only to be whirled back to the trail in the grip of the scorching leather.

The kid whooped and yelled, his mount kicking dirt and stones in its nervy excitement. Grisly-face growled, stepped forward from the twitching team and planted the toe of his boot firmly into Will's midriff. The whip curled again, cracked on the air like a pistol shot and coiled itself round Will's left leg, dragging him across the dirt in a suffocating cloud of grey, bone-dry dust.

Will groaned, grunted, choked, spat sand and grit and then the first globules of blood.

'Mealy-mouthed sodbuster!' quipped grisly-face, planting another kick before the whip swished and cracked again.

'One of yuh secure that wagon and team, damn it,' shouted the man with the whip. 'And get that Winchester.'

The kid slid from his mount and did as bull whip had

ordered, slapping his thighs and whooping at the top of his piping voice as he circled the horses. 'Now don't you go finishin' him before I've had my share,' he called, giggling at the sight of Will's face fast turning to a smudged blur under the smears of blood and dirt.

It was a full twenty minutes before the three men stood back exhausted, lathered in sweat, snorting like bulls, and stared at the near lifeless body of Will Petty.

'He ain't goin' no place,' wheezed grisly-face, wiping his brow. 'We bury him here?'

'That old creek-bed back of us there is the place,' croaked bull whip. 'Be nothin' but a pile of bones time anybody gets to findin' the body.'

'Want me to do it, then?' grinned the kid, his crystal eyes gleaming. 'Put a bullet in him – hell, it's gotta be my turn.'

Grisly-face spat. 'No shootin'. Never get to knowin' who might be prowlin' them hills. Don't want no nosy-parkers lookin' in.' He spat again. 'We drag the fella to the creek back of our mounts. He'll be dead in an hour, and then, my friends, we head for Miriam, sell the sodbuster's outfit and go treat ourselves at the Dollar Bit. What yuh reckon?'

'Fine, just fine,' beamed the kid. 'I got a hankerin' for that peachy redhead I saw there last fall. You remember her?'

'Sure, sure,' soothed bull whip. 'Let's just clean up here, eh?'

They lashed Will's ankles with the bull-whip, mounted up, grisly-face driving the outfit, and trailed slowly across the open dirt spreads and parched mesquite to the creek, dragging the body behind them. Once there, and with barely another word spoken between them, they stripped Will of his blood-soaked clothes, belt, holster and boots and kicked him down the rocky slope to the creek bed.

'Rains are due in about a week,' murmured bull whip, shielding his eyes against the glare as he scanned the empty skies. 'Wash the last of the sonofabitch down to the gulch. Won't be nothin' to see of him in a month.'

There was nothing then to mark the fate of Will Petty save the black scratches of circling buzzards on the cloud-less blue.

The summer rains came early that year, soaking the dusty land and filling the dry creek beds weeks ahead of the seasonal average – and it was because they were early that Eli Cornpaw got caught, as he put it, 'between the Devil and the downpour' and literally dragged a man from the brink of death.

Eli had been trailing his weatherbeaten prairie schooner due west for close on three months when he came to within a mile of the creek and judged that he had little more than a couple of hours before the rain clouds that had been travelling with him best part of the day emptied their promise right there. Time, he had reck-oned, to seek shelter; somewhere close. A rocky overhang along the line of the creek, he had decided.

It was chance, of course, that brought him spitting and cursing and cajoling his reluctant horse to the overhang within yards of the slope down which Will Petty had been bundled. And it was only chance that made him turn, once horse and schooner had been settled, to see just where it was he had finally holed-up against the now driving rain.

Seconds later he had spotted the naked body sprawled face-down in the fast-filling creek.

It took Eli close on a half-hour to ease, lift, part drag, part push and roll the body from the creek bed, into the rocks, through the cloying sand and dirt, to the dry ground at the overhang.

'Can't say as how I can do a lot for yuh, fella,' Eli had muttered through his toothless gums, blinking the rain clear of his eyes as he squelched and oozed round the body, 'but I'll give it my best shot. Yuh sure as hell look to be in a bad way there, but I figure for you still breathin' – just – and soon as I've got to lightin' some sort of fire here. . . . Meantime, let's dry yuh off and get you under blankets. God alone knows how you ever came to this.'

It was dark by the time the fire was lit and the soft flames licking on the easterly wind. The warmth, though doing a deal of good for the old man and the schooner horse, hardly stirred so much as a finger on the blanket-bound body.

It had been night for Will Petty, it seemed, for days.

There was a weak, watery moon streaked by scudding rain clouds on a whipping wind when Eli twitched awake, cursed quietly at the aches in his old bones and propped himself carefully on one elbow.

The rain had eased to a drizzle, the air cooled and grown thinner and the darkness filled with the sounds of the new flow rushing through the creek bed. The flames at the fire were low and twisting to the wind; white ash lifted in sudden clouds and spiralled across the night; the schooner horse snorted quietly as if dreaming.

Eli blinked, rubbed his stubbled chin and stared at the body in the shadowy glow of the fire. Fellow was still breathing, sure enough, and maybe there was a touch more colour in his cheeks. But, hell, he was clinging on there like a drowning man clutching at straws. It would take no more than the night chill, or a surge of damp, and he would be gone. In fact, it would be a miracle if he got to see sun-up.

The old man struggled from the comfort of the blanket, came to his feet and crossed to the pile of brush and timber he had stacked in readiness for fuelling the fire. He built on the flames, cleared the dead ash, stirred the embers to a fresh draught, then went in search of more blankets.

'Warmth,' he mumbled, 'got to have warmth. . . .'

Eli stayed at Will's side, tending him, bathing his brow when a fever threatened and finally broke in a lather of heat, then chill, until the body was a shuddering mass of torn flesh, cuts and bruises. He soothed in answer to the groaning, murmured to the moans, tried where he could to catch the few jumbled words that creaked through Will's lips, and, when he could summon his own strength, whispered a prayer.

'Don't seem a deal else for it, does there?' he whispered to himself. 'Guess the Good Lord'll know what to do. You just bank on it, fella.'

But it was almost first light on a day that was still wet and driven on a cutting wind when Will Petty opened his eyes wide and seemed for the first time in days to see a world that was no longer a nightmare.

'Well, now,' smiled Eli from his watchful seat by the fire,

'ain't you just a sight for a pair of sore eyes?' He adjusted the rough sacking covering his shoulders. 'Darn fool question, I know, but how yuh feelin'? Don't answer! Can see for m'self. Should be able to, damnit. Been watchin' over yuh best part of the time since I dragged yuh stark naked as the day you were born from that creek down there.'

The old man spat, smacked his lips and tended the pot simmering on the glow. 'Got some fresh coffee comin' along here. Say when you're ready. Grub too when you can take it.' He blinked and peered closer. 'Name's Eli Cornpaw, by the way. I ain't nobody special. M'self, the old nag there and my schooner been driftin' slowly west some long whiles. Figured that by the time I finally get there – wherever it is – I'll be old enough, grey enough and worn enough to find me some shade and put my feet up. Beginnin' to look that way too! Still, lucky for you I happened along of that creek, eh? You bet! Yessir. . . . Say, now you're stirrin' some, is there anythin' I can get yuh?'

'A gun,' croaked Will, staring into the old man's astonished eyes. 'Just a gun.'

THREE

The rains lingered long and heavy that year under skies that seemed forever full and dark and fit for no more than men to gather round fires to tell their tales.

Eli listened patiently and carefully to Will Petty's story, taking it just as and when he chose to relate it, watching the man's strength grow in the telling, as conscious of the healing of the fellow physically as he was of his resolve mentally. But it was some days before he finally put the question bothering him most.

'Done the best I can for you, Will,' he said, late one night as they relished the warmth and comfort of the fire in the overhang, 'but I figure for the rain clearin' come sun-up tomorrow and I guess you'll be for movin' on. Yuh don't look to be much right now in them old two-bit clothes of mine and them toe-crunchin' boots I dug out for you, but you're alive and that's what it's all about come the call.'

His eyes had narrowed. 'You'll want to smarten up at Miriam, eh? Get yourself a decent outfit, a horse, wagon mebbe. . . . Oh, don't you fret, I'll help you out best I can

16

with whatever cash I got. Sell up my own outfit. Sure I will. I trust yuh, and yuh sure as hell deserve another chance at whatever it is you've a mind to. And you'll pay me back when you can, know you will . . . assumin' o'course, you're still alive.'

Eli had waited then before putting the question. 'You still plannin' on trackin' down them scumbags who took your outfit and left you for dead? You still want that gun? You settin' out to kill them fellas? That the way of it, Will?'

Will had stared into the dancing flames. 'Owe my life to you, Eli. No doubtin' to that. Would've been a scatterin' of rain-washed, buzzard-picked bones down that gulch by now if it hadn't been for you. But I ain't for lettin' them rats go free, not no how I ain't. I wanna know who they are and where they are. And I'm beginnin' in Miriam. That's where they would've headed, and there's gotta be somebody there who'll know where they went.'

'Oh, sure, there'll be somebody, there always is. And you'll go chasin' out of Miriam on some whim of a rumour, and then there'll be somebody else, some other place, and on and on . . . and you ain't never goin' to know when to stop 'cos you mebbe ain't never goin' to get the chance.'

Eli had rummaged in his pockets for the remains of a part-smoked cigar, lit it and blew the smoke to the night. 'I seen it before, mister,' he added quietly. 'A sight too many times.'

'Yuh ain't suggestin' I forget these past days are yuh?' Will had frowned. 'Just pretend they never happened; walk away and let the scumbags ride on free to the next trail, the next lone wagon? That what yuh sayin'?'

'Not as such, I ain't – but, hell, we ain't been holed-up in these rocks fightin' for your life for you to go puttin' it right on the line again first chance yuh get. And that's what it'll be, mister. The odds ain't changed none. It'll still be three guns to one come the showdown.'

Will had gone back to staring into the flames.

Eli had sighed and smoked the cigar silently for a while. 'Still,' he had said at last, 'I guess it's your life and you've got every right to live it any way you choose. That's a fact, and seein' as I ain't for arguin' other, we'll pull out at first light and turn the wheels for Miriam.'

'You ain't committed to go no further. That understood?'

'Understood,' said Eli, his tired eyes twinkling behind the drifting cigar smoke.

Grace Keene laid aside her hairbrush, stared for a moment into the dressing-table mirror and wished, not for the first time that night, that she could wash away the face paint, the powder, the perfume, tie her long red hair in a ponytail, rip herself out of the cheap, tarty dress and pull on a pair of buckskin pants and her favourite old shirt and put the flea-bitten Dollar Bit and the town of Miriam far behind her.

As it was, another five minutes and she would close the door on her room, glide seductively down the stairs to the already crowded saloon bar, smile knowingly at the waiting customers, brush aside their groping paws, and for the next four hours be the all-time, good-time saloon bar girl.

It was a living and she hated every minute of it.

But tonight, she decided, patting the falls of her hair

across her bare shoulders, things might be different if the stranger was still in town.

He had arrived, along with his ageing partner, a worn prairie schooner and a horse long past its best, four days back, booked into Ma Kitchen's rooming-house, quickly bought himself some new clothes and boots at Charlie Tippett's mercantile, a second-hand Colt at the gunsmiths, and done a tight deal on a clear-footed roan mare at the livery.

It had been two days before he got to asking the questions.

Deputy lawman, Mac McLean, had been among the first to loosen his tongue on what had happened that particular morning at the sheriff's office. . . .

'Fella walked in bold as a brass-eye, that old-timer along of him, and said as how he was Will Petty and wanted to see Sheriff Cole on a matter of bushwhackin', theft and attempted murder. Just no messin'. Said as how the culprits – three of 'em he described in detail – had probably been holed-up awhiles right here in Miriam.'

'Hell, that would've been Rope Porter, Stiffkey and that wet-nosed kid Johnny Twist, who rides along of 'em,' said a man at the front of the listening group. 'Did the fella say their names?'

'Said as how he never heard names mentioned. They just beat him senseless, stripped him, left him for dead and drove out his wagon and possessions.'

'And that,' quipped another man in the gathering, 'would've been the outfit Porter sold on to them travellin' folk passin' through here a time back.'

'Anyhow,' McLean continued, 'this fella Petty said as

how he wanted to know where the bushwhackers had headed. Sheriff Cole explained he didn't know. Porter and his boys had never hinted.'

The men murmured among themselves for a moment. 'Just pulled out, didn't they?' said the man at the front again. 'Left before first light. I heard 'em go, but never saw 'em. Seemed to be ridin' west. But to where? Hell, that's gotta be anybody's guess. . . .'

But not for everyone. Grace Keene knew exactly where the trio had been headed. Johnny Twist had told her.

FOUR

The smoke haze lingered like a slow mist; the smell of liquor, stale, fresh and cheap, crept round the bar as if looking for somewhere to hide, only occasionally swamped by a bar girl's perfume or a customer's weeks of crusted trail dirt.

The level of noise at this time of the early part of the night in the Dollar Bit saloon remained at a steady level; the low hum of general talk, bouts of belly laughter, some chuckles, giggles, the slap of a hand to flesh, shift of bottles across tabletops, clink of glasses.

Store owner, Charlie Tippett, had a low stakes poker game gathering momentum in a far corner; Sheriff Cole and his deputy, Mac McLean, were drooling over the pleasures of a blonde and a brunette at the bar, the level of the newly opened bottle of 'best in the house' whiskey between them falling rapidly.

Saloon proprietor, Blake Winter, waited expectantly at the foot of the stairs to the balcony rooms, a flaking of cigar ash dusting the brocade of his waistcoat, his jewelled fingers working anxiously, his eyes flitting like caged birds from the bar and its comings and goings, to the batwings, the low glow of the town lights on the night, then back to the stairs, the darkened balcony and the closed doors to the rooms.

One of them was about to open. Any second now, he thought, flicking open the engraved lid of his timepiece. Grace was religiously punctual. She could be relied on, trusted. She was an asset. Perish the day she ever decided to saddle-up and leave. Not, of course, that he would allow it: Grace Keene owed everything to Blake Winter.

A door opened. A shaft of light fell across the balcony. The bar fell silent.

'Evenin', Miss Keene,' greeted Sheriff Cole, tipping his hat as he stepped to the foot of the stairs and extended a hand to Grace. 'Pretty as a picture as ever, if I may say so,' he smiled. 'Can't imagine what this town's done to deserve such a treasure.'

Grace returned the smile, glanced quickly at Winter and then anxiously through a long gaze over the crowded bar.

'Looks like bein' a busy night,' beamed Winter, dusting the ash from his waistcoat. 'What I like to see. Good for the town, eh, Sheriff?'

Cole stayed silent, his eyes fixed on Grace.

'Strangers about?' asked Grace casually.

'Few travellin' folk, miss,' said Cole. 'Nobody special.'

'Mr Petty and his friend still in town?'

'Still here,' grinned the sheriff. 'Still hopin' he can dig somethin' up on Rope Porter and his sidekicks, but like I told him —'

'I think Mr Tippett is tryin' to attract your attention, my dear,' smiled Winter, taking Grace's arm. 'We shouldn't keep him waitin'.'

Grace nodded decorously and moved away, the stares following her like a flock of hungry birds, unaware of the face at the batwings and the creak of them as Will Petty stepped into the bar.

'Get yourself along of me, gal. I'm in need of a lucky run!' Charlie Tippett's arm locked on Grace's waist, pulling her to his side at the gaming table. 'And somebody go get the lady a drink. Nothin' cheap.'

Grace winced at the manhandling, restored her smile, but turned her gaze beyond the table to the bar and the man working his way slowly to its far end. She watched Will Petty until he was settled with a beer in his hand, hoping she might catch his eye for a moment, make some sign to indicate she needed to speak with him.

No such luck, damn it. He was too intent on watching the sheriff.

'Now you just get to plantin' them luscious lips of yours on this hand of cards I got here, Grace, and let's see 'em scoop this pot!' Tippett thrust the cards into Grace's face. She brushed her lips lightly across them and smiled thinly to the whoops and cheers of the watching men. 'Let's play!' beamed Tippett, tightening his grip on Grace's waist.

'Yuh don't own her, do yuh?' growled a voice among the smoke.

Grace tensed. Tippett hesitated, his arm easing back to the table. The noise level dropped. Sheriff Cole's eyes narrowed. Cigar ash tumbled to Blake Winter's waistcoat.

'Who's askin'?' snapped the storekeeper angrily.

A thick-set fellow, with a lazy left eye and a scar across his neck, stepped into the brighter glow of light, slung his weight to one hip and glared at the poker players. 'Me,' he drawled. 'I'm askin'.'

'And who the hell is "me" when he's in town?' grinned Tippett, his gaze tightening. 'I don't readily bring you to mind, mister.'

'Don't count none, does it?' said the man, the lazy eye twitching. 'T'ain't you I'm interested in.'

The bar customers tittered. Winter began to sweat. Grace glanced quickly to where Will Petty was finishing his beer. Sheriff Cole and his deputy ushered the bar girls to the shadows.

'Easy there, fella,' ordered Cole. 'Ain't no cause for a dispute here. Plenty of girls available.'

'Sure there is,' grinned Winter. 'Why, we got some of the prettiest girls this side of —'

'I'm askin' about the lady there,' clipped the man, his gaze still tight on Tippett.

'Well, now,' began Winter again, 'Miss Keene is always happy —'

'She's along of me right now,' snapped Tippett. 'And that's where she's stayin' 'til I say other.'

The man shifted his weight. 'So you do own her?' he drawled.

'I just told yuh, mister —'

'Nobody owns me,' flared Grace, stepping away from the table, her fists clenching. 'None of you. Not one.'

Winter's mouth opened and closed. Sheriff Cole's hand

eased softly to the butt of his holstered Colt. A bar girl began to sniff and shiver. A drunk rolled his eyes and slapped his lips.

Tippett laid aside his cards, pushed back his chair and came slowly to his feet. 'That's it, then, ain't it?' he smiled. 'You heard what the lady said: nobody owns her. Made it clear enough. No doubtin' to it. So why don't we have ourselves a drink and just get to coolin' this down some? I'm buyin'.'

'Hold it,' growled the man, the lazy eye steady and focused. 'I don't take much to the tone of you, mister. You somebody special hereabouts? You got a stake on all the women in town?'

'Now you see here,' began Tippett as the other players left the table, 'I ain't for havin' —'

'I seen and heard all I wanna see and hear. You bet I have!'

The man's first shot from his fast-drawn Colt burned deep into the storekeeper's arm as he reached instinctively for his gun. The second blaze, ripping through the sudden clatter of bottles and glasses, scraping of chairs and tables, thud of boots on floorboards, screams of the bar girls, shouts and curses, threw Charlie Tippett across the bar as if in the whip of a hurricane.

The man swung away to the batwings, his gun blazing shots into Sheriff Cole's shoulder and spinning his deputy across the bar. He glanced only once at Grace, the lazy eye brightening like a moon, then turned to dive through the 'wings.

But he never made it and died from a single shot in a pool of blood a body's length from the boardwalk.

When Grace dared to open her eyes, Will Petty was standing over the dead man, his secondhand Colt still in his hand.

FIVE

'Darn me, I leave yuh to yourself a couple of hours, and what happens? You're into a shootin' faster than it takes to spit it out. Trouble stalks you, Will Petty, like your own shadow! And that's the truth of it.' Eli Cornpaw pushed his hat from his brow and scratched his head. 'Sooner we get the dust of this town behind us, the better.' He pulled the hat into place. 'Who was the fella yuh shot, anyhow?'

Will steadied his mount as he smoothed a saddle blanket across the mare's back. 'Nobody I knew,' he murmured quietly. 'Just got himself into a mess back there and paid the full price for bein' a murderin' fool. No sayin' how many more he would've taken out.'

'Yeah, well, lucky for you the sheriff agrees. Seems like he's a deal grateful for what you did . But that don't change nothin' of the facts, and one of them bein' that the time's come to trail on, with or without any notion of where them rats who robbed yuh happen to have headed. We agreed on that?'

Will moved across the livery to collect his saddle.

'Agreed,' he said, lifting the leather in his arms, 'but that don't mean —'

'And before you say it, I ain't lettin' you go alone. Yuh just ain't safe! Might fall foul of anythin'. In fact, you most certainly will!' Eli mopped a bandanna round his neck. 'I ain't sold up everythin' I own to see it all blown away in cordite. Nossir. Givin' up that prairie schooner of mine; puttin' the old nag out to grass . . . bits and pieces sold for dollar bits . . . why, that's a whole lifetime sold out for you, Will Petty, and I've half a mind —'

'Make it a full mind, old-timer, and stay,' said Will, slinging the saddle into position. 'There ain't no call for you to be involved any deeper in this. I'll pay back every last cent I owe you. And some. All you gotta do is put your feet up and take it easy 'til I get back. Few weeks at most.'

Eli blinked and screwed his face into sunburned wrinkles. 'Stay here – in Miriam?' he scowled. 'Put my feet up in this two-bit, sand-fly town? Mister, you would have to rope me down on agreein' to a darn fool proposition like that. I ain't ready for the shady porch life, not yet I ain't. And 'sides, I prefer to keep a close eye on a fella owin' me money, specially when he's as sure-footed prone as you are for findin' trouble! So you'd best get used to havin' me around.'

The old man smacked his lips and narrowed his eyes. 'Talk around town this mornn' is that the fella you shot never so much as saw you draw on that Colt you got there.' He waited a moment. 'Where'd you learn to shoot like that?'

Will continued to saddle up the patient mare.

*

'He's fast, believe me. I saw it all,' said Blake Winter, with a nod of authority to Sheriff Cole. 'Watched every move the fella made, and I tell yuh straight up, I sure as hell wouldn't want to be facin' him in a showdown. Any sane fella would want Will Petty, whoever he is, on his side.'

Sheriff Cole winced at the throb of pain in his heavily bandaged shoulder and stepped carefully across the still cluttered saloon bar of the Dollar Bit to the batwings. The morning in the dusty street had dawned warm and clear, but strangely silent in the aftermath of the night's shooting.

'Right there, right where you're standin',' nodded Winter again to the sheriff's back. 'That's where that sonofabitch died, thanks to Will Petty.' He grunted and dusted the brocade of his waistcoat. 'Pity he didn't shoot sooner. Charlie Tippett might have lived, and that deputy of yours wouldn't be lyin' useless in his bed.' Winter came wearily to his feet from the table and crossed to the bar. He ran a finger through the stains and huffed irritably. 'Goin' to take days to get this place cleaned up decent. And all because of some half-drunk, womanizin' sonofabitch. . . . Hell!' He sighed. 'Will Petty still in town?'

'Saddlin' up right now,' murmured Cole. 'Be gone before noon, the old-timer along of him.'

'Pity. Town could do with the likes of him around. Chasin' after that Rope Porter scum, I suppose? Waste of a good man's time. Porter will be long clear of the territory by now. North, south . . . east, west. . . . Who's to say? Fellas of his cut don't announce their plans exactly. Will Petty will be lucky if he ever sees the man again. But if he does – well, now, that might be real interestin', judgin' by what we saw here last night.'

Sheriff Cole turned slowly from the batwings. 'Fella ain't for bein' persuaded other, that's for sure,' he murmured. 'He'll go his own way. Mind of his own.' He glanced quickly at the stairs to the balcony. 'How's Grace this mornin'?'

'Grace is Grace,' smiled Winter. 'She'll be fine. You'll see her tonight, you can bet to it.'

Grace Keene turned the key in the lock of the door, listened for a moment, assured herself that the balcony beyond the room was deserted, smiled softly and decided that now was the time. There would never be a better opportunity.

She crossed quickly to the battered luggage trunk in the corner of her room, lifted the lid through its grating squeak, and delved anxiously among the contents. Buckskin pants, the much-loved old shirt, tooled leather belt, boots, hat . . . they were all there, just as she had folded them what seemed now a lifetime ago. She took them out, laid them aside and delved again, this time to the bottom of the trunk and into the right-hand corner.

Her fingers closed nervously on the oil-cloth package and sensed the shape beneath the weave. She had inherited the Colt when her pa had died and the homestead out Ohio way been sold up. The gun, cleaned through and polished once a week, had hung on the living-room wall in its buffed leather holster throughout Grace's life at their home. But she had been taught to load, aim and fire it.

'Some folk reckon to a woman havin' no good cause to handle a piece like this,' her pa had said. 'Mebbe so, and God-willin' you never will, but I'm a pragmatic old devil and I figure for havin' raised yuh to face life as it is. It sometimes don't discriminate too kindly between male and female. So, who knows, day might dawn when you'll be mighty glad you heeded your pa's gun lessons. . . .'

And this, thought Grace, taking the package of the Colt and holster in her grip, was that day.

Fifteen minutes later, she was dressed in the pants and shirt, had pulled on the boots, strapped the holstered Colt at her waist, and donned the hat. She took a last look at herself in the dressing-table mirror, glanced quickly round the familiar room, and crossed back to the locked door.

She listened carefully again. She could hear the drone of Blake Winter's voice in the saloon bar, the occasional grunts from Sheriff Cole; otherwise the place seemed quiet enough. The bar girls would be sleeping off the night's exertions, the cleaners awaiting their orders from Winter, the town drunk still snoring.

But she knew exactly where Will Petty and his partner would be.

There had been no chance of coming close to the man following the shooting in the bar, and she would have to wait, she had decided, on another opportunity of telling what she knew of Johnny Twist and outlining the deal she had in mind.

But then the rumours of Will's departure had started to circulate and Grace had made her final decision: she would find the man at the livery, put her proposition and be clear of Miriam by mid-afternoon. Will Petty, she believed, would have no choice but to listen to her and agree to her plan.

She stiffened at a knock on the door and the grate of a weary voice.

'You there, ma'am? Best get yuh butt shiftin' sharpish. Winter wants you. Urgent, he says.'

Grace bit at her lower lip. 'Who is that?' she asked.

'Tay Preston, ma'am.'

'Thought I recognized the voice, Tay,' said Grace lightly. 'You got a minute there?'

'Well, I. . . . Sure, I guess so, ma'am,' murmured Preston hesitantly. 'But Mr Winter seems like he's in some hurry.'

'He can wait a moment,' answered Grace. 'Just give me a hand here, will you?'

She unlocked the door quietly and let it swing slowly open, the Colt already raised in her hand as she waited for the sight of a head.

SIX

Tay Preston had never seen more than the door closing on Grace Keene's room. Hell, it was more than a fellow's life was worth to come to the threshold, let alone step inside without a proper invitation. But she had said for him to come in, so here he was, hat in hand, steps as soft as a fly's across creamed butter.

Tay's thoughts in those next moments were a jumble of images of the room, its furnishings, the dressing-table, the dress laid across the bed, the fancy decor, quality carpeting, and he might well have caught a heady whiff of perfume, maybe lavender.

But he would have seen nothing of the sudden glint of the Colt above his head, the tight grip of slim, anxious fingers, the swing of the arm that brought the barrel of the gun crashing across his skull.

He went down with a thud and a groan that finally died on a bubbled hiss.

Grace stepped back, catching her breath, her eyes wide and round, sweat gleaming on her brow. She stared at the man sprawled at her feet, stepped over him and held the door to within an inch of closing, listening for the softest movement, the first approaching footfall.

Nothing. All clear. She would shift, right now. She glanced at the unconscious man again. 'Sorry about that, Tay,' she murmured. 'No offence intended.'

Seconds later she had left the room, closed the door softly behind her and inched her way along the corridor to the back stairs. Once down them and into the clutter of barrels, crates and boxes at the rear of the Dollar Bit and she could move quickly through the shadowed places to the livery.

But how long, she wondered, before Tay Preston stirred or Blake Winter's patience snapped?

'And here's another thing for you to get to mullin' over,' said Eli, slapping his lips adamantly as he adjusted the girth on the saddle of his mount. 'Supposin', but only supposin' mind, that we get to the trail of them bush-whackin' scumbags, and just supposin' we come to within a lick-spit of where they're holed-up, how in tarnation we ever goin' to take 'em out, or have you got some sono-fabitch scheme for bringin' 'em to book with the law? And if that's the case, mister, then I for one ain't thinkin' straight.'

'Will you just hold up on the supposin' there awhile?' grunted Will, from where he stood in the shadows at the open-sided end of the livery. 'I figure for us havin' some company headin' this way.'

'Company?' smacked the old man, easing to Will's side. 'Now just who in tarnation. . . .' He screwed his eyes against the glare of the sun and peered harder. 'Say, ain't that the frills and fancy gal from the Dollar Bit? Takes some recognizin' under that dude outfit. So what's she doin. . . . Damnit, you're right, she is headin' this way and makin' a whole meal of stayin' out of sight along of it. Why?'

'I think we're about to find out,' murmured Will, stepping back.

They waited in silence, close in the shadows, watching carefully as the woman threaded her way like a scurrying insect towards the livery. She paused wherever she found shadowed cover to take stock of her bearings, glance hurriedly back to the saloon, assess the way ahead, then move again, low and fast.

'Got herself some fast-shootin' piece there,' murmured Eli, his eyes narrowing. 'And what's the bettin' she knows full well how to use it?' He smacked his lips on a grunt. 'One helluva town, ain't it? Just never know what it's goin' to throw up next. Still don't figure, though, why the gal is in such a darned hurry.'

Another minute, another twisting, diving run and Grace Keene was into the livery and looking anxiously, breathlessly around her.

'Wouldn't happen to be lookin' for me, would you, ma'am?' said Will stepping into the brighter light.

Grace turned to face the voice, her gaze sharp but startled, the Colt tight in her hand. 'Will Petty?' she croaked drily.

'That's me, ma'am,' smiled Will. 'But easy with the piece there. I ain't spoilin' for a fight, especially with a lady.'

'Sorry,' said Grace, holstering the Colt. 'Touch nervy

here, and I ain't got a lot of time. Name's Grace Keene. You've maybe heard of me.'

'And seen yuh, ma'am,' smiled Will again. 'Why, me and my partner, Eli here —'

'I know all about you and your friend,' interrupted Grace, glancing back to the still quiet saloon. 'At least, I know enough . . . about what happened to you back there on the trail.' She paused, her stare on Will sharpening. 'And I know most of what there is to know about the men who bushwhacked you.'

Will stiffened. 'You wouldn't happen to know —'

'Where they were heading from here? Sure I would. For reasons I won't go into right now, I came to know Johnny Twist, the one they call the Kid, very well. He told me where the three of them were heading out of Miriam.'

'Then perhaps —' began Will.

'But there's a deal on here, Mr Petty. I'll come straight to the point: you get me out of this town and let me ride along of you, and I'll tell you exactly where Rope Porter, Stiffkey and Johnny Twist are holed-up. I want out of Miriam, but it's going to have to be fast. There's a fella back there at the saloon who'll be coming to with a nasty head any minute now, and the man who thinks he has an all-time stake in me, Blake Winter, isn't going to be one bit pleased with my behaviour when he gets to hear.

'What you see here is what you get: just as I am, no baggage and right now no horse. So what's it going to be, Mr Petty? Do we have a deal?'

'Hell now, mind if I get a word in here, seein' as how I got a vested interest?' said Eli, smacking his lips as he pushed dramatically at his floppy broad-brimmed hat.

'Seems to me we might have somethin' of a problem. One, I ain't seen hide nor hair of the livery fella here all mornin', so just how we goin' to get a horse saddled up for you *and* pay for it . . . you tell me.'

'We help ourselves,' snapped Will, turning back to the view at the open end of the stabling. 'Pay for it later when we've settled with them scum.'

'We?' frowned Eli. 'When *we've* settled with Rope Porter . . . you countin' the lady in on this?'

Will glanced at Grace. 'Am I?' he asked.

'If that's in the deal and I get out of Miriam, then that's it,' said Grace.

Eli sighed, smacked his lips, then slapped his thigh. 'Darned if I ain't heard everythin' now. Lady, you must either be one hell desperate to clear this town, or mad as a sun-fazed dog! And I wouldn't wager which!'

Blake Winter thudded a fist to the plush baize-covered table in his private quarters at the Dollar Bit and glared like an angered animal at Sheriff Cole. 'Not only an ungrateful, low-bit schemin' whore, but a horse-thief along of it. We could hang her for horse-stealin', that fella Will Petty and the old-timer either side of her!'

The sheriff squirmed uncomfortably in his chair at the table and drummed the fingers of one hand on the smooth surface. 'Why'd she up and leave?' he asked almost casually. 'Why go to all that trouble; take the risk? She that desperate?'

'Bitch!' seethed Winter, stalking across the room to the window overlooking the cluttered rear of the saloon. 'Who was it found her trail-scuffin' with the likes of Sol Peet and

Charlie Smythe; who was it cleaned her up, fed and watered her, dressed her decent and kept her that way?' He turned sharply. 'Who made her the Queen of Miriam, answer me that?'

'Well, I guess —' began Cole.

'I did, damn it!' glowered Winter. 'Hadn't been for me she'd still be a dirt-cheap, trail whore. And maybe that's how she'll finish up again.'

'Doubt that.' The sheriff's fingers lay still. 'No, I figure for her havin' some information on Porter and his side-kicks for which Mr Will Petty was ready to pay a high price. After all, Grace spent sometime with that kid, Johnny Twist. He had a mouth as loose as a clapboard in a high wind. He'd talk, tell her where it was Porter was headed.' The fingers stretched. 'That was the information she traded for ridin' out with Petty. She struck a deal.'

'Mebbe, but she ain't goin' to get away with it. Not no how she ain't. I can't afford it. The Dollar Bit can't afford it; this town can't afford it. Grace Keene is irreplaceable, and that's a fact. Admit it.'

The sheriff shrugged and nodded. 'So?' he asked, wincing at the throb of pain in his bandaged shoulder.

'So we go after her,' grinned Winter, dusting the lapels of his waistcoat.

'Now hold on there. I ain't so sure —'

'You raise a posse, say half-a-dozen good men, myself included, you headin' it up, and we ride hard and fast and for as long as it takes 'til we find Grace and bring her right back to where she belongs: here, under my control.'

Sheriff Cole came brusquely but painfully to his feet. 'I can't go raisin' a posse on the pretext of bringin' a whore back to where she works. T'ain't the law.'

'True,' smiled Winter. 'But raisin' a posse to bring horse-thieves to book is very much the law, ain't it?'

SEVEN

They had ridden fast and hard from the livery at Miriam on the trail heading due north high into the sprawling mass of the Long Feet Hills, and held the thundering pace until close on noon when lathered mounts, aching limbs and the swirling dust on parched throats brought them to a halt in the shadowed lee of rocky overhangs.

'So far, so good,' spluttered Grace clearing the dust from her face. 'No hint of being followed.'

'Not yet,' spat Eli, pushing at the floppy brim of his hat. 'Only a matter of time, ma'am. I don't figure for the owner of that livery back there, the sheriff or that Winter fella takin' kindly to you skippin' town – or to us for helpin' yuh come to that.' He glanced at Will. 'Ain't I just right, mister?'

Will Petty shrugged and slid tiredly from his mount. 'Mebbe,' he murmured. 'We got a head start, which is somethin'.'

'O'course, it'd be a whole heap helpful if we knew just where exactly we're headin',' snapped Eli, with a wry slap of his lips. 'Care to tell us, ma'am, or yuh still sittin' tight on that?'

'North,' answered Grace bluntly. 'That'll do for now.'

'Sure know how to cut a deal and still hold all the cards, don't yuh, Miss Keene?'

'Had good cause to learn fast in the profession I've had to follow, Mr Cornpaw,' smiled Grace. 'What you know is sometimes all you're worth. Isn't that so, Mr Petty?'

Will turned from tending his mount. 'I'm trustin' to you, ma'am, and I'm hopin' you're trustin' to me. Should be by now.' He gazed beyond the slopes from the overhang to the spread of the far horizon. 'Another ten minutes, that's all we can spare, then we push on. Guess you'll be the best judge of when and where we hole up for the night, ma'am.' His eyes gleamed in their quick, penetrative glance. 'I'm reckonin' on you givin' us good warnin'.'

Grace nodded. 'Grateful for what you've done, Mr Petty, and, yes, you will have good notice of our night stop.'

'Well, ain't that just dandy!' mocked Eli, smacking his lips again. 'You two go on bein' as polite as this to each other and we'll be dressin' all dude-fancy for dinner!' He slapped his thigh. 'Let's just stay with the ridin' and watchin' our backs, eh?'

Blake Winter finished the careful loading of his Colt, spun the chamber and slid the piece thoughtfully to the holster on the gunbelt laid across the baize-topped table.

Time for its use would come soon enough, he decided, on a quiet grunt, as he turned and crossed through the soft lantern glow of his room to the drinks cabinet. He poured a generous measure of whiskey, sipped at it and turned again to stare at the gun.

Been a while since he had used it, he reflected, but he knew how. You bet. He might look a typically frock-coated saloon owner, but there had been a time. . . . Well, best not get to reminiscing on that; it was all he needed now that Rope Porter's tongue had been loose enough for long enough on a bottle of best whiskey for him to reveal his plans for a proposed raid on the bank at Kearney.

He took another sip of the drink and smiled gently to himself. Events since Porter's night of his loose tongue had created an unusual situation: Grace Keene's bid for freedom was the almost perfect excuse for riding to Kearney and, with care and timing, taking a share of the bank haul for the asking.

It would be some raid, big by Porter's standards, but it might just work in a town like Kearney. And if it did, he pondered, would he make two hits with one shot, so to speak: the capture and return of Grace Keene to the Dollar Bit, plus a share of the bank haul?

Grace had spent some time with the equally loose-lipped Johnny Twist and almost certainly learned that he, Porter and Stiffkey were headed for Kearney. That would have been her bargaining card to play to Will Petty in seeking his help to see her safely out of town; she would ride with Petty in his quest to settle the score with the bush-whackers.

But had Grace also learned of the planned bank raid?

Winter finished the drink in a single gulp and stared blankly into the green baize, his mind racing through likely events, the way to play things with Sheriff Cole and the posse that would pull out of town at first light.

He would say nothing of Porter's plans, but suggest almost casually that they head north. 'Might be as well to make Kearney our first objective – woman like Grace won't survive rough country for long. She'll be hankerin' for a town soon enough,' he would suggest, and with any luck Cole and the others would buy it.

And once into Kearney. . . .

He broke the reverie on a brisk grunt, turned and went back to the drinks cabinet. If Rope Porter was to be believed, a large deposit of gold was due to arrive in Kearney from the Bedrock Mining Company in about five days. Porter would strike once the haul was clear of the heavily guarded wagons and into the bank. But he might find he had an uninvited partner to reckon with.

A week at most from tomorrow, pondered Winter again, and the world might be a very different place. He might even decide to head west with Grace Keene at his side. Make a fresh start; keep the woman – *his* woman – in the style she deserved. He would, after all, be able to afford it.

He poured another measure of the best whiskey and relished it with an air of warm anticipation.

Eli watched the curl of smoke from the night fire swirl like a veil across the face of Grace Keene. Not for the first time since the thin flames had seared the darkness, he noticed the woman's eyes, green in this light, sharp as thorns, penetrating, watching him as a hawk might stare through mist at a mouse.

He wafted a hand across the smoke and cleared his

throat. 'Mite thoughtful there, ma'am,' he said, taking the mug of coffee in both hands. 'Lot to think about, though, pullin' out like yuh did. Bet they never thought back there in Miriam —'

'I'm just glad to be out, Mr Cornpaw,' clipped Grace, shifting uncomfortably on the hard rock seat. 'And very grateful to Mr Petty for his help,' she added, glancing round her. 'Where is he, by the way? He seems to have been gone some time.'

'Well, now,' said the old man, leaning forward to the fire for a taper to light a cheroot, 'that's mebbe somethin' you're goin' to have to get used to if you're plannin' on stayin' along of us awhiles. You see, Will there don't take over kindly to the dark, specially when he's in open country. Figures yuh can just never tell what it might be hidin'.' He lit the cheroot and tossed the taper back to the flames. 'If yuh follow me, ma'am.'

Grace's eyes narrowed for a moment. 'Of course,' she murmured. 'He went through a bad experience. Things like that can scar a man for life.'

'So right now, this very minute,' continued Eli, drawing heavily on the cheroot, 'he's takin' a long look out there just to make sure we ain't bein' spied on by some no-good, two-bit drifter or the likes. Guess he wants to make certain we all get a good night's sleep. . . . Assumin', of course, we've still got some ways to ride.' He blew a twist of smoke. 'Would that be so, ma'am?'

Grace smiled and adjusted the strap of her hat. 'Don't give up, do you, Mr Cornpaw? Still pondering on our destination?'

'Well, put it this way, ma'am, an awful lot seems to

have happened since that rainy old day when I stumbled across a half-dead body down in that dirt trail creek. Not that I'm complainin', mark yuh. Nossir. Sold up my outfit to raise some cash willingly enough, and I ain't for desertin' Will Petty at the drop of no hat, not 'til I seen him through whatever it is he's gotta settle in him. And that, ma'am, with all due respect, is beginnin' to depend very much on you and that conversation you had with that Johnny Twist scum.' Eli drew on the cheroot again. ' 'Sides, a fella gets to my age he likes all the notice he can summon on where he's headin'. He ain't much for wild-track wanderin'.'

Grace's steady stare deepened through the veil of smoke.

'But I figure I've mebbe worked it out, anyhow,' said Eli, haughtily.

'Oh,' frowned Grace, 'and how's that?'

Eli smacked his lips and studied the glowing tip of the cheroot. 'Due north out of Miriam into the Long Feet Hills, accordin' to my reckonin', puts you on a course for the minin' camps at Silvertown. They don't seem to me to be the sorta places Rope Porter would have a hankerin' for exactly. On the other hand, there's Kearney.' He paused a moment to draw on the cheroot. 'Now there's a waggin'-tail town; sorta set-up might just suit Porter and his partners. Girls, gamblin', easy-goin' outlook on the law. . . . Yeah, I reckon Porter would go for Kearney. What do you reckon, ma'am?'

Grace's smile freshened as she came to her feet and crossed to her loose-hitched mount. 'You could be right at that, Mr Cornpaw. But all I'm reckoning right now is that it's time to turn in.' She turned and reached for her bedroll without another word.

The night air had thinned to a keen chill when Will Petty finally stepped silently from the deeper darkness to the shadowy glow of the fading firelight and eased to a seat at the old man's side.

'I ain't for sleepin', Eli. We got company out there. Two by the sounds of 'em, settled close. No proper sight yet. I can just smell 'em.'

Eli simply nodded and glanced fearfully at the sleeping woman.

EIGHT

They came through the first drift of dawn like something smudged across the light. Two men, tall, slow-moving, watchful, with steps that seemed to barely scuff the dirt as if walking on water, arms and hands relaxed, dustcoats pushed back to display holstered twin Colts.

Mean, trail-weathered types, thought Eli, eyeing them without blinking as they approached at the same measured pace, step for step, yard by yard, silently, their gazes tight. Men without shadows at this hour of the day.

'Easy there, ma'am,' murmured the old man, taking Grace's hand, his lips slapping softly on his toothless gums. 'Don't say nothin'. Leave the talkin' to me. And don't look round for Will.'

'Where is he, for heaven's sake?' hissed Grace. 'Why isn't he here?'

'How do you know he ain't?'

Grace tossed her loose hair nervously. 'I just hope —'

'Watch the light, ma'am. That's all yuh got to do. Watch the light.'

The men began to slow, their shapes darkening, eyes

47

gleaming. One of them spat deliberately into the dirt ahead of him. His partner's cheek twitched on a jumpy nerve.

A hitched mount snorted and stamped a hoof. Grace's fingers hardened in Eli's hand.

'We ain't much for standin' to ceremony,' said the man on the left, coming to a halt with his partner. 'And we ain't got the time, so we'll get to it.'

'Only thing you'll be gettin' to, mister —' growled Eli, his glare defiant under the floppy brim of his hat.

'No lip, old-timer,' snapped the man on the right. 'We ain't for takin' it. All we want is the woman there.'

Grace stiffened on a shudder and began to sweat in spite of the dawn chill. Eli scuffed a boot and smacked his lips loudly. 'Yeah, well, that may be so, fella,' he growled again, 'but my guessin' would be for the lady herself havin' somethin' to say on that.' He straightened his shoulders. 'She's with me and stayin' that way. No more to be said. Best get your day started and ride on.' The men were silent, unmoving for a moment, their hands still, their stares like white lights. The spitting man spat again.

The second man merely let a grin of amusement spread to a smile. 'Feisty with it, ain't he?' he drawled, dropping his weight to one hip. 'Kinda early for it, too. Could get to givin' me a sore head, and a sore head just ain't on my schedule for this day, not when I'm takin' in the likes of the lady there.' The smile faded. 'You're spoilin' the view, old man. Yuh know that? You hearin' me loud and clear?'

Eli mumbled and grunted, but held firm to Grace's sweating hand as she tossed her hair dramatically and levelled her stare.

'Now we get to doin' this real civilized,' said the spitting man. 'Hell, t'ain't no big deal, is it, f'Cris'sake? Old slappy lips here ain't got no legit' right at his age to be holdin' a lady like yourself, ma'am – that's as obvious as day comin' up. Don't know how he came by yuh, but me and my partner are sure goin' to be happy and comforted to be liberatin' yuh from him, and that's for hell-fire sure. Ain't that so, Harb?'

The second man grinned and grunted, as his gaze scanned the softly breaking light.

'Harb agrees. So here's how we settle the deal.' The spitting man hawked and spat. 'Me and Harb here are figurin' for trailin' dead-eyed south for the long plains into Mexican country. Warm nights, wine and shady verandas and all that. And you, lady, are comin' with us.'

'You're goin' to have to shoot me first,' croaked Eli, easing a careful step forward.

'You can bet to that, old-timer!' grinned the spitting man. 'But you got my word on it, we'll make it quick.'

Grace's eyes narrowed as she stared across and through the still growing light. Where was Will Petty, she wondered, what was he waiting for? She shivered as the spitting man moved towards her.

'Stand aside there, fella,' he quipped, gesturing at Eli with an outstretched arm. 'Time for dealin' with you ain't quite here yet. Meantime, I'm for takin' a closer look at the lady.'

Eli had taken another step, coming directly into the path of the spitting man, when his partner drew quickly on one of his twin Colts and levelled it menacingly into space.

'Three mounts,' he grated. 'How come? Why they got three horses loose hitched?'

The spitting man halted, touched the brim of his hat as his gaze focused on the horses, then shifted slowly, tightening on the suddenly fierce glare of the rising sun.

'Well,' he asked, staring at Eli, 'why three?'

'One's a pack,' said Eli hurriedly. 'Trail horse.'

'That ain't no pack,' clipped Harb, spinning the Colt through his fingers. 'That's a ridin' horse. So where's the rider?'

Grace shivered and tossed her hair. Eli smacked his lips.

'I said where's the —'

'Right here.'

Will Petty's voice snapped through the thin, chilled air, the glaring light as if cracking it like glass. The spitting man squinted, trying with one hand to shield his eyes against the blazing sunlight, fumbling uselessly with the other over the butt of his Colt.

His partner, Harb, his gun already drawn and cleaving the air, made to bring the weapon into a levelled aim, blinked on the blinding light, cursed, twitched and fired a shot high and hopelessly wild.

It was to be the last shot the drifting, trail-stained gunslinger ever fired as Will's Colt blazed a single, searing flash of lead that flung the man back to the dirt in a whirl of arms and legs.

Grace Keene screamed, her eyes swimming, body suddenly limp under Eli's heave against her, crashing her to the ground. The spitting man snarled, cleared his Colt from its holster in a jumble of sweat-soaked fingers, but never brought pressure to bear on the trigger.

He twisted, gripping his gut under the rage of shots from where Will stood his ground, back to the light, the glare of the morning silhouetting him to a thrusting shadow of his shape.

It was all done, the spitting man and his partner sprawled dead, in what seemed to Eli only seconds. He blinked on the swirl of dust, swallowed and came unsteadily to his feet, pushed his floppy hat to the back of his head and reached to help Grace.

'Told yuh, didn't I?' he murmured. 'Told yuh to watch for the light. Came out of it like a ghost. . . .'

'Kearney.' Grace Keene spoke the word as if clearing the last of a bad taste from her mouth. She shivered, folded her arms across her breasts and stared hard and deep into Will Petty's face. 'That's where you're headed – and I'm coming with you. All the way.'

'Said as much, didn't I?' smiled Eli, smacking his lips. 'Just darn well knew it'd be Kearney. It figured.'

Will turned to gaze for a moment over the twisting hill trail to the north. 'Obliged to yuh, ma'am, and you can take it myself and Eli will see you safely there. After that —'

'Heck, Will, it don't need no spellin' out after what we've just witnessed,' snapped the old man, pulling fiercely at his hat. 'There's no way Miss Keene here can be left to an open trail. Territory's probably riddled with the likes of the scum you've just consigned to the dirt they deserve. She wouldn't get to within a spit of Kearney, would she? 'Course she rides with us, and we make darn certain she's settled before you go drawin' on that Colt

again.' He grinned. 'Where *did* yuh learn to shoot like
that, damn it?'

Grace rubbed her shoulders against the chill. 'I'm just
glad. . . .' She shivered again. 'Just grateful. Shall we ride?'

'You bet,' said Eli. 'Put some distance between us and
whatever that saloon-keeper back in Miriam is plannin'.
Sheriff's probably raised a posse by now.'

Will's gaze tightened on the trail. 'Why Kearney?' he
murmured to himself, a frown darkening his brow. 'You
wouldn't figure it for a first choice so far north.'

'It's sure as Sunday got its share of the rough life,' said
Eli. 'I seen it once, way back. Tell yuh somethin', when
them Silvertown miners hit the place, wow, yuh ain't seen
nothin'! Them fellas raise hell like there was no t'morrow.'

'Hmm,' pondered Will. 'But that still don't tell us why
types the likes of Porter, Stiffkey and Johnny Twist want to
be there.' He turned to face Grace. 'Twist give any reason,
ma'am?'

'Nothing I've got cause to recall,' shrugged Grace. 'He
just said it was Rope Porter's plan to head there. Made it
sound as if Kearney was as good a place as any.'

'Heck, let's just get there, eh?' said Eli. 'We ain't
learnin' nothin' standin' here.'

Grace nodded and moved towards her mount, her
quick glance at the bodies of the dead gunslingers vague
and hesitant on another shudder.

Eli waited until the woman was out of earshot before
turning sharply to Will. 'Fella steps outa the light like you
did there, mister, didn't learn it by chance,' he quipped,
one eye watching Grace. 'You don't fool me none. Only

next time, don't leave it so late! I was beginnin' to think I was goin' to have to settle with them scumbags m'self!'

NINE

'That man Petty's handiwork. Plain as the nose on your face, Sheriff.' Blake Winter stood back from the stench and sight of the dead bodies and dusted the lapels of his frock-coat with pernickety care. 'Clean shots. No messin'. That's got to be Petty.'

Sheriff Cole grunted quietly, as he broke from the three men at his side and stepped forward for a closer look. 'I ain't disputin' it,' he said, his nose twitching. 'Couple of drifters, and nasty-lookin' with it. No great loss, I'd reckon.'

'Agreed,' nodded Winter, 'but you see the significance, don't you?'

The sheriff frowned and scratched his head. 'Well —' he began.

'The significance bein', Sheriff, that here we are, miles clear of Miriam on the main trail headin' north with two cheap but very dead gunslingers who have met their grisly end at the hand of Will Petty. Now, why did they so upset Mr Petty, do you suppose? Because, of course, of the woman, Grace Keene. They would have loved to have gotten their grubby hands on her. You can bet to that!

Alas, they died – but we know, one, Grace was here, and, two, that she, Petty and the old-timer continued north. Headin' where?' He paused, eyeing the sheriff watchfully. 'I would wager Kearney.'

Cole rubbed his chin. 'Kearney,' he muttered. 'You could be right at that. Town's the sort of place Porter and his boys would make a real meal of: girls, booze, gamin'. . . . And no decent law to speak of, not that I'd rate, anyhow. Yep, I'd go along with Kearney. But what the hell is Grace goin' to find there?'

'She's just ridin' at the moment, ain't she?' said Winter. 'And I don't suppose she gives a damn where she's headed. But we'll catch her. Oh, yes, we'll be there when the time comes.' He broke the reverie and grinned. 'So, do we continue to Kearney, Sheriff?'

Cole turned to the three men. 'What yuh say, fellas? We ridin' for Kearney?'

The men talked quickly among themselves. 'Kearney it is,' said their spokesman. 'Grace is worth it!'

'You've got your answer,' smiled Cole.

Winter examined the state of his fingernails. 'Your decision entirely, Sheriff,' he murmured, his gaze gleaming. 'I was merely makin' suggestions, you understand. But I think you're right. Kearney has to be our destination, and if we make good progress through the rest of this day and mebbe – only mebbe, mark you – do some night ridin', why . . . coupla days and we could have this whole thing sussed through and Grace back safe and sound and on her way home. Yes, indeed.' He adjusted the set of his coat and crossed to his mount. 'You made a good decision there, Sheriff. Sound thinkin'.'

Cole nodded an acknowledgement. Decision-making had always been his strong point, he reflected.

'We holdin' to this track? Gettin' worse by the foot.' Eli took the reins to his mount in a tighter grip as he persuaded the horse a few more steps along the narrow ledge trail, then fixed his gaze on the woman ahead of him. 'Easy as yuh go there, ma'am. There ain't no hurry.'

He risked another quick glance to his left and the sheer drop to rough brush and sage. His stomach churned and turned cold. He blinked and glanced to his right and the towering, smooth-sided rock face reaching to craggy peaks.

'Don't know about you folk,' he grunted, 'but I don't have much of a head for heights. Same go for you, Will, or ain't you fussed?'

'Soon be done,' answered Will, concentrating on his own steps and guiding his mount. 'Just watch the way ahead.'

'Darn sight easier said than done!' Eli shook the sweat from his face and cursed quietly at the glaring sunlight. 'What yuh reckon, ma'am? Bet you wished you'd stayed back there at the Dollar Bit, eh?'

'I've been in more hospitable surroundings, that's for sure,' gasped Grace. 'But as for the Dollar Bit . . . it can fry in hell! If taking this track cuts the miles and gets us to Kearney that much quicker, we'll do it.'

'Well, I'll say this for you, ma'am, yuh ain't short on guts,' said Eli, urging his mount on. 'And they're sure as hell bein' put to the test, what with them trail rats we had back there and now this. And God alone knows how deep the rattlers' nest comin' up. I tell yuh straight, a comfortable bed under a decent roof gets to soundin' mighty appealin', and like I'm tellin' yuh, I ain't got no head —'

The sudden clattering beat of wings and high-pitched screeching drowned the old man's voice as a panicked buzzard flared into life from a ledge on the rock face.

'What in the name of —' growled Eli, only to be stifled again by his snorting, bucking horse and the screams of Grace Keene.

'Hold on there, ma'am,' yelled Will, grappling to hold his own balance.

The buzzard continued to screech and flap its wings wildly in its panicking state, finally dragging its talons across Grace's shoulder.

Eli had collapsed to his knees in a breathless heap. Will reached to grab the reins of Grace's mount. The buzzard erupted in a wheeling swoop of broken feathers and dived away on a suddenly gentle cruise to the lower tree heads.

But Grace had already lost her footing.

Eli watched, still on his knees, his mouth open, eyes glazed, as Grace grabbed at empty space, missing Will's outstretched hand by a breath. She seemed then to be suspended for a moment, neither balanced nor falling, until, in a whirl of limbs and tossing waves of her hair, she toppled from the track and fell soundlessly, almost timelessly, out of Will and Eli's sight into the trees and brush far below.

The silence that followed gripped like the heat.

It took Will and Eli a full hour of struggling back from the narrow track to the main trail and searching out a route into the brush and trees before they were able to begin the search for Grace.

'Hell's teeth,' sweated Eli, 'it's askin' an awful lot to expect her to still be in one piece. Fact is, she might not even be alive.'

'I know that well enough,' groaned Will, forcing a path between the bodies of trees and the tangles of scrub.

'Should never have taken to that ledge. Should've stayed with the trail.'

Will heaved aside a fallen branch. 'We were all of the same mind. We took the chance.'

Eli smacked his lips and dodged the whip of a frond of brush. 'Yeah, and look where it got us.' He grunted and adjusted his hat. 'Yuh see anythin' up ahead there?'

'More of the same. Thick as a mangrove swamp.'

The old man gasped, took a deep breath and shielded his eyes as he gazed over the sheer rock. 'We were about there,' he said, pointing to the high track. 'Woman fell in a straight drop, so that would mean she should have hit about. . . .' He peered ahead, his hand tracing the fall. 'I'd reckon about there. Dozen yards ahead of yuh.'

'I got it,' said Will, struggling on.

'But I ain't one bit hopeful,' Eli added hurriedly, shaking a bandanna from his pocket to mop his face. 'Heck, place like this is about as remote as you can get. Reminds me of them forests out Colorado way. You bet it does. Why, I once spent close on a whole week tryin' to find my way back to where I'd started! And you know what —'

'This place ain't that remote,' muttered Will. 'Look here.'

He held aside a tangle of growth to reveal a scuffed, flattened area where bodies – more than one, maybe three – had arranged bedrolls, lit a small fire between stones and loose-hitched their mounts.

'Drifters,' said Will.

Eli stepped to the blackened area of the dead fire and squatted. 'Still warm,' he murmured, running the ash through his fingers. 'Whoever was here ain't been that long gone. In fact —'

Eli gulped and stared through a lathering of hot sweat as Will turned from the shadows beyond the clearing, a torn remnant of Grace's shirt in his hand. 'Is she there?' he gulped again. 'Yuh see a body?'

'Nothin',' murmured Will, staring at the limp cloth. 'No sign of her, savin' this.'

Eli came slowly upright. 'Well, if we ain't got a body, but we've got the piece you're holdin', and we know for a fact that somebody was holed up right here, then I'd figure —'

'Same as m'self,' said Will. 'That there's a fair chance the fellas here found Grace and have taken her God knows where.'

Eli mopped his face with the bandanna, blinked furiously, and scratched his grey stubble. 'Kearney?' he ventured. 'That's about the only place worth headin' with a woman who's goin' to be in need of a doc before very long. So what do you reckon?'

Will continued to stare at the remnant for a moment, then tightened and narrowed his gaze on the surrounding scrub and trees. 'We'll take a look around, see if we can find any tracks. If Grace Keene is still alive and whoever's

found her is headed for Kearney, we'll pick up the trail
and go get her whatever it takes.'

However long it takes, pondered Eli, behind the
sodden bandanna.

TEN

Kearney had grown fast in the wake of the Silvertown mining boom. What had once been scant more than a collection of ramshackle huts and lean-to outbuildings huddled in the dirt like old men on their knees, had blossomed into a town that boasted gambling, girls, saloons, mercantiles, a top trail livery serving the stage-line north, a bank and a full-time sheriff with sworn deputies.

Gold and silver were at the very heart of Kearney. They were its pulse and its blood and, inevitably it seemed to some, its disease.

Livery owner, Bart Parnham, had been among the early settlers to the area, building his small-time homestead into quality stabling and a prosperous smithy. Bart was also a spokesman for those who had long since feared the decline of Kearney into lawlessness.

'Ain't no argument concernin' the bounty of riches sittin' up there in them hills,' he had argued, 'and I ain't got nothin' but admiration for the good men who give their lives to hackin' it out – mebbe it's all God's will, mebbe not – but I sure as hell don't take kindly to some of the consequences.

'Seems to me we're gettin' to attract just about every hollow-legged drunk, every two-bit gunslinger, all the drifters in creation and every loose-livin' scumbag – male and female – you can imagine. That's gold for yuh, and I don't see no way of stoppin' it, but I'd sure like to reckon on the law hereabouts makin' it possible for a fella to sleep easy in his bed of a night.

'That's what we need, folks: decent law and order, all day, every day. And that is precisely what we ain't got. Seems to me just about anybody out of anywhere can ride into this town at any time of his choosin' and nobody gives a damn. . . .'

Like today, thought Bart, wiping his hands on the rag from the pile at his side as he watched the approaching riders through the curling smoke from the forge. Three of them heading into town from the southern trail out of the Long Feet; two men, dirt-scuffed drifters, some long miles under their belts, and a woman who looked to be in a bad way.

Now from just where, he wondered, had this unsavoury threesome started out? Who were they and where were they headed? No two guesses what they needed, he reckoned: a doc for the woman. And fast.

'Howdy,' called the leading rider, reining his mount to a halt upwind of the smoking forge. 'Yuh got a decent doc hereabouts? Lady here sure could use one.'

Bart eyed the man carefully. Tall in the saddle, but lean and looking in need of a square meal behind a hot bath, he thought. His partner, just as lean and hungry-looking, wore a patch over one eye.

'Doc Marley,' said Bart. 'Far end of town. Clapboard house on your right. Can't miss it.' He glanced anxiously at the woman. 'She looks real bad, mister. Yuh come far?'

The one-eyed man hawked and spat. 'Far enough,' he croaked out of a dry, dusty throat. 'And we ain't for wastin' any more time.'

Bart shrugged and reached for another rag from the pile. 'Stablin' here's cheap enough when you're ready.'

The riders nodded and grunted and pulled at the line to the woman's horse bringing her face on to Bart for a brief, agonizing moment as he took in the cuts and bruising on her face and neck, bedraggled hair, torn shirt, hanging left arm, and the gaze of dazed bewilderment in her swollen eyes. Her lips, dragging to one side, moved only once in her stare into Bart's face, but there was no sound, he could decipher.

In the next minute the three were no more than dark smudges in the drifting smoke from the forge, and Bart was shaking his head. Typical, he thought; folk just ride in, strangers, no count taken of who they are, where they come from; might be anybody set to do almost anything.

But hell, he pondered, throwing aside the rag, that woman had looked to be real sick. Somebody should get to asking how it was she had come to be in that state.

Johnny Twist stirred in his chair on the long, shadowed veranda fronting the Gold Rush Saloon and pushed the brim of his hat from his eyes. He yawned, flexed his arms, stretched his legs and grimaced on the bitter taste of cheap whiskey in his mouth.

Time would come – and soon, he reckoned – when two-bit saloon sourmash would be a thing of the past. He would drink only the best, the finest, come his days of leisure and lazing in the hacienda south, and maybe have a couple of hot-bloodied *señoritas* to pour it for him. Sure he would.

Meantime, there were new arrivals in town.

He sat fully upright, wiped a hand over his sweat-streaked face and narrowed his gaze on the riders making their slow way along the main street, their sprawled shadows thickening in the late afternoon light.

'Scumbags,' he murmured softly, grimacing again on the sour taste. Find their likes almost anywhere on the trails west; scrounging types; lift the corn from granny's plate without a second thought. But there was some-thing different about the rider being loose-rope trailed behind the others.

You bet there was. A woman. And, damn it, he knew her! That mound of dirt and rags, lolling head and dazed, near-unconscious gaze, was no less than the famous Grace Keene, star turn at the Dollar Bit in Miriam, the very woman whose bed he had shared what seemed only days back. What in the name of hell was she doing here in Kearney in that state, with a pair of the roughest-looking trail drifters he had ever clapped eyes on?

He came watchfully to his feet, taking care to stay deep in the shadow, his mind already racing with thoughts of Rope Porter and Stiffkey's reactions to what he was about to tell them. He swallowed and backed carefully to the batwings as the riders passed.

The sourness in his mouth tasted like poison.

'She needs rest and plenty of it, and a whole heap of nursin'. In a state of numbed shock, darn near to coma here. You'd best leave the lady in my care. I got a back room I can fix up.'

Doc Marley, moved closer to peer carefully and swab tenderly at Grace Keene's cut and bruised neck, disregarding the impatient shift of boots from the two men at his back. 'Where'd you say you found her?'

'We didn't,' said the man with a patch at his eye. 'And she won't be stayin' – not here, anyhow.'

Doc swung round sharply, pushing his spectacles back to the bridge of his nose. 'I'm tellin' you fellas —' he flared.

'We heard yuh first time, Doc,' clipped one-eye's partner. 'But just do the doctorin', will yuh, and we'll take care of the rest.'

'Take care?' flared Doc again. 'Why, I doubt if you'd have the first notion of how to set about nursin' the lady.' He turned back to Grace. 'Be days, mebbe weeks, before she's anythin' like back to normal. Bruises, cuts, sprains, an arm here that's in real bad shape, and no sayin' to the internal injuries she's sustained. Damnit, she's driftin' in and out of consciousness like there was no time.' He patted Grace's hand as he continued to clean her cuts. 'Who is she? She give yuh a name?'

'Not yet, but she will when she gets to realizin' what

we've done for her,' murmured one-eye. 'I figure for her bein' real tough.'

'Oh, she's that all right,' said Doc. 'Tough as they come. That's why she's still in one breathin' piece, but from here on. . . . Just what are you fellas plannin' to do with the lady? Where you goin' to take her? And, bearin' in mind you don't even know her name, supposin' she don't go along with your plans? Could be she'll be all for biddin' you a big good day.'

One-eye's fingers flexed over the butt of his holstered Colt. 'Like we said, Doc,' he drawled, 'just get to the doctorin', eh? Patch the lady up, real good, quick as you can, and give your tongue some rest. Yuh got it?'

Doc scowled, pushed at his spectacles and continued to tend Grace. 'Law hereabouts might have somethin' to say on this matter,' he mumbled just loud enough to be heard. 'And you might get to ponderin' who was travellin' with the lady. I wouldn't reckon for her bein' on her own out there, wherever you found her, would you? And when she comes to havin' a clear head and ain't in a state of shock like she is now, she's goin' to have plenty to say. Plenty! With me right along of her. And you can bet to that!'

'Here? In Kearney? Grace Keene?' Rope Porter eased his empty glass to the table and stared hard into Johnny Twist's eyes. 'That ain't possible, is it?'

'Right there in the street with them scumbags trailin' her in like a dog,' sweated Twist. 'No mistakin'. I been too close to that woman not to know her, but she ain't lookin' in no sort of health.'

Stiffkey, seated on the other side of the table, poured himself another drink from the half-empty bottle. 'She might be a problem,' he murmured, drumming his fingers across a faded whiskey stain. 'She'll have to be taken care of.'

Porter leaned back in his chair. 'The problem bein', of course, that fella she worked for: Blake Winter.' He swallowed noisily. 'He'll be certain to come chasin' after her, draggin' no tellin' how many guns behind him.' He shifted uneasily. 'Loose guns around town we don't need.'

Stiffkey's fingers flattened on the table. 'Odd, ain't it?' he said quietly. 'Odd that Grace Keene pulls out of Miriam – Lord knows how or who she was with – and odder still that Winter might be figurin' in our thinkin' again, 'specially at a time like this when we've got our lives laid on the line for a big raid.' He grinned at the others through his slow, searching gaze. 'I just hope that neither of you got liquored up and loose-lipped in your conversations at the Dollar Bit. Yuh didn't, did yuh?'

' 'Course not,' spluttered Twist. 'Who would? Hell, we ain't that stupid.' He licked at a beading of sweat. ' 'Course we didn't,' he laughed.

Porter squirmed again. 'Here's what we do,' he grunted drily. 'We wait 'til dark, then we go find the woman; get rid of the scumbags holdin' her.'

'And what do we do with her then?' asked Twist anxiously. 'Hell, we ain't for no way killin' her, are we? That'd be a real waste.'

'No, we ain't for no killin'. We go batten her down at that deserted shack we passed on the way here. We'll collect her later, when our bankin' business, so to speak, is done.' Porter smiled. 'Consider her a sorta bonus. How about that?'

'Hey, I like it!' grinned Twist. 'I like it a lot. Good thinkin' there, Rope.'

Stiffkey finished his drink. 'Grace Keene wouldn't have left Miriam alone, and she wouldn't have left with no two-bit trail drifters neither. So who got her clear of town and Blake Winter's hold on her? And a sight more to the point at issue, where is he now?'

Porter came to his feet. 'You're worryin' to no cause, my friend,' he scoffed lightly. 'Shift your butt there and let's go watch the sun go down!'

ELEVEN

Sheriff Otis Crabbe eyed the two men watching him from behind a thick cloud of drifting smoke. They were both upstanding, honest-to-God citizens the pair of them, he thought, easing more smoke from between his stained teeth, but he could well do without their meddling.

'So,' he said, his barrel-chest swelling, 'you patched the woman up best yuh could in the time, then you let her go. That the way of it, Doc?'

'Had no choice, did I?' frowned Doc Marley, pacing to the window of the sheriff's office. 'Them scumbags weren't foolin'. They'd have shot me right there if I'd tried anythin'. Important thing was to fix the woman.'

'And did you?' pursued Crabbe.

'Cleaned her up, but she was still only semi-conscious; in a world of her own. She never said a word, and probably won't 'til she's had some proper sleep and rest. And Lord above knows where's she goin' to get that.'

'Any idea where the men took her?' asked Crabbe. 'She still in town?'

'They ain't booked into rooms no place. I've checked,'

69

said Bart Parnham, stiffening his shoulders importantly. 'But they'll still be here. Got to be. My figurin' would be any one of them old huts and barns far end of town.'

'But just what are they plannin' to do with her?' grunted Doc, peering through the window at the steadily darkening street and thickening shadows.

Sheriff Crabbe drew on his cigar again and blew the smoke to another cloud. 'Sell her when she's fit enough to be sold,' he announced bluntly. 'Fetch a high price out Silvertown way. Them minin' fellas are always on the look-out for a fresh face.'

'Well, we ain't goin' to allow that to happen, are we?' huffed Bart, thrusting his thumbs into his braces. 'Not no how, we ain't. That just ain't right.'

'Agreed,' said Doc. 'Can't be a party to no such thing. So we'll go find the poor soul; raise some fellas; put a search party together. We'll show them scum-trailin' varmints —'

'Whoa there! Ease up,' gestured Crabbe, raising his arms. 'I'll do the figurin' and plannin' round here. Can't go chargin' round the town like a herd of sore-belly bulls. We got to get organized.'

'So organize, f'Cris'sake!' snapped Bart. 'We're wastin' good time here. Woman could be dead for all we know.'

Meddling town folk, thought Crabbe, behind a still thicker cloud of cigar smoke. His meeting with Rope Porter would have to wait.

The sheriff was true to his word: he organized and had a dozen town men, including himself and a deputy, Doc Marley and Bart Parnham, gathered outside his office and awaiting instructions within the hour.

'Now we know what we're lookin' for,' he said, with a piercing military glare over the assembled men, 'and we got some idea of where the woman might be holed up. So we go to it, but we don't go rushin' and blunderin' – and I don't want to hear any shootin', not in my town without my say-so. Yuh all got that?' The men murmured their understanding. 'Let's get this done.'

The search was systematic, much to Bart's surprise, as he remarked to Doc. 'Otis ain't usually this sober when it comes to keepin' the law. What's with him – he taken the pledge or somethin'?'

'Mebbe he's coolin' down some in his middle years,' Doc grunted. 'Whatever, I ain't fussed, just so long as we find that woman before it's too darn late. Should never have let them rats take her like they did. Should've stood my ground. Just hope I did enough to keep her goin'. . . .'

They were deep into the search through the jumble of disused buildings at the rear of the main street, the glow from their lanterns probing into dark, shadowed places that had not been disturbed in years, when Charlie McGraw saw the trail of blood, and then, at the back of a ramshackle hut, discovered the bodies.

'Over here, Sheriff,' he called across the night. 'I found the scumbags. Dead as stone. But no sign of the woman.'

It was not the state of the bodies, the glazed, staring eyes, open mouths, that chilled Doc Marley's spine as he knelt at Crabbe's side to pronounce that the drifters were indeed dead; it was the loss of the woman that raised the cold sweat on his brow.

'One knifed, one strangled,' he murmured, coming

upright again. 'No scuffle, no sounds, not so anybody would notice. But these scum ain't the point. The point is, where's the woman? Whoever did this, took her. But why, and where are they holdin' her now? She must've still been alive when she left here, but I wouldn't like to say for how long she's goin' to be able to hold on.'

'We need to keep lookin',' insisted Bart from the gathering of men. 'We got the men; we're all willin' enough. Time we took this town apart, went in search of the real scum we've let move in over the months.' The men nodded and murmured. 'That woman's got to be around here some place. She can't just disappear, not again. But it's a whole sight more important that we lay our hands on the fellas who did this. There ain't no place in Kearney for out-and-out murderers. Ain't that so, Sheriff? Ain't that what we got to do?'

Sheriff Crabbe could only grunt and order that somebody go rouse the undertaker.

Rope Porter melted into the night like a shadow as he crossed the unlit alley, skirted a sprawl of empty crates and barrels and came to the shape waiting for him in the darkness.

'We're goin' to have to make this quick,' hissed Sheriff Crabbe, his eyes wide and watchful, his face wet with sweat. 'I got a jumpy town waitin' on me. Goin' to be some time before they settle.' His gaze danced anxiously for a moment. 'Them killin's and the disappearance of that woman anythin' to do with you and your boys by any chance?'

'We got a special interest in the woman,' murmured

Porter quietly. 'Crossed her back in Miriam. But don't you fret none. We got her safe, outa town, and she'll be taken care of – one way or the other. Just you keep concentrated on your side of our bargain.'

'No problems. Gold will be in the bank here in a couple of days.' Crabbe smiled softly. 'I'm personally overseein' its safe deposit.'

'I like that,' grinned Porter. 'Make sure you do a good job.'

'Meantime,' persisted Crabbe, 'what about that woman? How come she was here in Kearney with them trail dogs? And how was it —?'

'Leave it,' snapped Porter. 'You ain't no need to worry. Me and the boys'll do whatever's necessary. You know what yuh got to do if you want that easy life you've been tellin' me about.'

'I just hope that woman ain't trailin' no baggage along of her,' hissed Crabbe, as he began to sidle away to the shadows. 'We'll talk again t'morrow.'

Porter watched in silence as the lawman slipped away to the main street, his thoughts turning again miserably through his recollections of a night of drunken indulgence in Blake Winter's private quarters at the Dollar Bit.

Just what, he struggled to recall, had been said through those long hours? How much had Winter taken in and understood? Where, damn it, was he right now?

He grunted softly on his thoughts, tapped the butt of his Colt and began to move away, hugging the deeper darkness and shadows against the lanterns and flares of the roving town men.

Time to be firmly indoors, he decided – which is where he hoped Johnny Twist was keeping himself back at that remote trail shack.

Was it a light; a shape flitting across it? Had there been a movement, a sound? Or was he getting spooked?

Damn it, this was no sort of a place to be for a fellow the likes of Johnny Twist. He had better things to be doing than nursing a half-conscious woman, more dead than alive, who simply stared into space and said nothing. Hell, a fellow his age should be out there, whooping it up with the Gold Rush girls. . . .

But had there really been a light out there?

He crossed through the gloom of the shack to the dust-smeared, cobwebbed window and peered into the night beyond. Dark as a dead man's boot, he thought, flicking his fingers over a drift of web; hard to see anything that had any recognizable shape.

The trio had stumbled across the long-deserted shack by chance on their way into Kearney. 'Make a note of it,' Porter had said. 'Might be a useful hole come a bad day.'

And so it had proved, but even so how come he had drawn the short straw to stand guard, making the best of such miserable comforts? Even the woman had been forced to use the floor with no more than a blanket for warmth.

Stiffkey had said he would take over the watch at dawn. Well, in that case the sooner first light got to showing itself the better.

There it was again – the light, something of a shape moving through it. But no sounds. Nothing.

He wiped a flush of sweat from his face, flicked again at the strands of cobweb and narrowed his gaze in concentration. He could go take a look out there, he mused, but that would mean leaving the woman and going against Rope Porter's orders: 'You don't stray from her side, not for nothin'. Nothin'. Yuh got that?'

He had it, so he would have to wait and watch, go without sleep, stand here at the window till his legs were as dead as the timbers round him.

Hell, how come a woman like Grace Keene had gotten herself into a situation like this? He would have credited her with a whole sight more good sense than to go trail-drifting beyond that fancy perfumed room of hers back at the Dollar Bit. . . .

The light! Closer now. Moving. There *was* somebody out there.

TWELVE

'Well, what do you reckon?' whispered Eli from the shadows. 'We ain't mistaken, are we? There's somebody there, and he's goin' to a mighty heap of trouble not to announce himself.'

Will Petty shifted his weight where he peered from the cover of tangled brush and rocks. 'There's a mount hitched in what's still standin' of that lean-to,' he murmured. 'Been there some time.' His gaze tightened. 'Light your cheroot again. Let's see if the glow shifts the fella.'

Eli struck a match and let the flame flare for a moment. 'Yep, he's movin', one side of that window to the other. Yuh see him?'

Will grunted as he scanned what he could make out of the surrounding shapes. 'That shack ain't been occupied in years, not on a regular basis. Roof's holed to the right, and that smoke stack's grown enough weed to fill your boots.'

'Small-time settler's place from way back,' said Eli. 'Some poor devil who finally got to figurin' there was more to be made pannin' and hackin' for a nugget of gold out Silvertown way than there was in scratchin' dirt for a measly crop.'

He pushed at the brim of his hat. 'We ain't that far from Kearney, so I'd reckon for the fella holed-up there bein' out of town or headin' there. Fact that he ain't burnin' a light and ain't for acknowledgin' ours kinda points to him wantin' to keep his own company. We that bothered? We could make Kearney come sun-up.'

'Just somethin' about that mount,' pondered Will. 'Set of its head; shape of the ears . . . flash of white on that fetlock. . . .' His gaze began to gleam and stayed unblinking in a sudden swirl of images. 'That day,' he croaked into space. 'The trail . . . them bushwhackers. . . .'

'Yuh sayin' that horse belongs to one of the rats who left yuh for dead?' gulped Eli. 'Yuh recognize it? But, hell, how —'

'Johnny Twist, the one they called the Kid.'

Eli ground the cigar to a dead stub at his heel and gulped again. 'You sure about that, Will?' he prodded. 'I mean, yuh could be mistaken in this light. Kid could have sold the horse on. But, hell, what would Twist be doin' here, anyhow, and alone at that? I wouldn't figure for the scumbag strayin' far from the others.'

'It's Johnny Twist all right,' murmured Will. 'I just got that feelin' it is. And the only reason he's out here in a place like this is because he's under orders – Rope Porter's orders – to be here.'

Eli smacked his lips softly. 'Mebbe. Ain't nothin' to say you're wrong. So what yuh goin' to do: sit it out 'til sun-up, or you figurin' on makin' a move right now? Fella don't know who we are, but he sure as fat turkey knows we're here. And you can bet your sweet life he's already fidgetin' on that.'

'We wait awhile,' said Will, his eyes narrowing darkly on the tumbledown shack. 'Let the sonofabitch fidget. Meantime, light yourself another cigar and relax.'

Damnit, whoever was out there was having the two-bit cheek to bed down for the night! Johnny Twist scattered the strands of the cobweb from the windowpane and pushed his face as close as he dared to the dirt-streaked glass. Fellow had even had the gall to light a cigar as if settling after a hot supper. Hell, he had half a mind. . . .

The woman stirred and moaned in the corner. 'And you'd best stay quiet if you know what's good for you, lady,' he hissed, turning quickly. 'I ain't for messin' with you, not while we got company out there.' He swung back to the window, his fingers closing instinctively on the butt of his Colt.

Maybe he could go take a quick look at who it was had taken to this patch of the territory for his bed. No harm done in looking; he could hardly be expected to spend all night watching and waiting. Chances were the fellow was no more than a trail-sore drifter, too broke and down on his luck to afford a room in town, bottle of sourmash his prized possession.

And in any case, he reasoned, Rope would thank him for checking out somebody approaching this close. Woman was going to be a whole heap valuable – a bank raid 'bonus' – come a few days' time. Rope wanted her in good shape once she was recovered from the treatment meted out by the scumbags she had fallen foul of. But they, he smiled, had been taken care of, so that left only the cigar-smoking drifter out there to check on.

How come a trail dog could afford cigars, he wondered?

He glanced at the woman – silent now and deep into sleep – peered through the window again and slid softly over the creaking floorboards to the door. He waited, listening, his gaze bright on the inky darkness, the fingers of one hand twitching at the butt of his Colt, his thoughts beginning to race.

Once through the door he would head for the cover of the thick, untamed bush surrounding the shack. He would stay hidden and wait, give the fellow out there the chance to make a move or sit it out. And when he reckoned the time to be right. . . .

One shot would do it. Fast and accurate. Drunken sonofa-nosy-bitch would never feel a thing. Probably pass on grateful to be out of his misery.

'He's shiftin',' murmured Eli behind a waft of smoky breath. 'Down there in the brush to your right. Got him?'

'Got him,' grunted Will, his gaze steady and focused. 'Freshen up that cigar. Let's keep the rat concentratin'.'

'Damn it, Will, these smokes don't come cheap.'

'Buy yuh a whole box when we're done. Now just light it and keep watchin'.'

Eli flared a match and blew smoke. 'He's lookin' but he ain't movin',' he whispered. 'Mebbe he's waitin' on us. What yuh reckon?'

'Curious, and perhaps just a mite uncertain,' answered

Will. 'But I ain't for reckonin' on Johnny Twist bein' an overly patient man. Give him a few more minutes – and keep that cigar smoke movin'.'

'And where in hell do you think you're goin'?' frowned the old man, behind another cloud of smoke. 'You ain't goin' to get to some fool schemin', are yuh?'

'Work my way towards the side of the shack. There's plenty of cover.' Will edged deeper into the shadows. 'You just keep that sonofabitch occupied with that smoke.'

'And you —' hissed Eli, but by then the man was lost to the night.

Eli grunted quietly, drew on the cigar and released a swirl of smoke. He waited a moment for it to drift on the thin air, then peered hard into the sprawl of brush and scrub hiding Johnny Twist.

Not a movement. Not a sound. You could hear a caterpillar's creep out there, he thought, as his gaze narrowed in its concentration. Say this for the fellow, he knew how to hide; sharp as a mountain lion, keen as a hawk. Probably been doing it most of his life. Came as second nature.

A slow crack of undergrowth, the shift of a shadow. 'Easy, Will, easy,' murmured Eli to himself, his gaze flicking anxiously to where he figured Will was moving.

Silence again. The shadows stiff and sentinel. Twist had not moved. Or had he, wondered Eli, licking at a sudden beading of sweat? Could be his patience had worn thin. Maybe he was not for spending the rest of the night stalking shadows.

Supposing he had something hidden in the shack that needed to stay hidden. Now that —

'You put so much as a breath outa place, mister, and it'll be your last.'

The voice at Eli's back hissed into the night like the spit of a riled rattler, the click of the Colt hammer chilling the sweat on the old man's neck to an icy bite.

Eli gulped and spread his arms, the cigar still smoking between his fingers. 'I ain't for interferin' none, fella,' he croaked. 'Just passin' through, headin' up Silvertown way, mebbe get m'self a stake, do some stream pannin'. You know the sorta thing.'

'So why'd yuh stop here?' hissed Twist again, the gun barrel prodding into Eli's neck as the gunslinger lifted the cigar from his fingers.

'Chance, just chance,' shrugged Eli lightly. 'Happened across the shack there, but could see it weren't much, so I —'

'I figure for yuh bein' a liar, old man,' drawled Twist.

'Liar? I ain't lyin'.'

'You're lyin' 'cos yuh ain't got to tellin' me about your partner. Yuh got two mounts here, mister, both saddled. So where's the other fella? And don't tell me he's catchin' up on his sleep.'

Eli swallowed noisily and smacked his lips. 'Well, now,' he began, 'I can explain —'

'*That won't be necessary.*'

Johnny Twist swung round, tense, tight, half crouched, his eyes wide and glaring, lips curled on a snarl that stayed locked in his throat. 'Who the hell's there?' he croaked drily.

'Can't yuh guess?' said Will, slowly, from the depths of

the darkness between scrub, brush, trees and rock. 'Don't tell me I've slipped from your memory already.'

Twist probed the Colt instinctively, at the same time snapping the fingers of his free hand for Eli to step to his side.

'Who in hell are yuh?' clipped the gunman, swallowing, beginning to sweat, his eyes narrowing as they peered for a shape.

There was a long moment of silence. Eli gulped and ran his tongue over his lips. Twist continued to stare, his eyes straining in their sockets for the slightest movement, anything that might offer a target for the Colt in his anxious hand.

'You goin' to show yourself, mister?' he croaked again. 'You got the guts to step from them shadows?'

'Oh, I ain't in no hurry, Johnny. I'm kinda relishin' seein' you fret there. And no sonofabitch Rope Porter or Stiffkey to help yuh out neither. Know how it feels to stand alone, eh? So do I, Kid, so do I . . . waitin' on a bull whip to crack . . . on the bite of it . . . then you can smell the blood, your own blood. T'ain't a pleasant smell, Johnny. Nossir, that it ain't.'

'What is this, f'Cris'sake?'

'Lone wagon and driver on the trail headin' south short of Miriam; hot, sticky day, but not long to the rains. You recall that day don't you, Johnny? You recall takin a likin' to the wagon . . . havin' y'self some laughs at the loose-lipped sodbuster's expense? Sure you recall.'

Eli gulped again. Johnny Twist simply stared and sweated, his throat tightening on every slow swallow.

'Hell, I was in a poor way by the time you threw me

naked as a babe into that dry-creek bed. You bet. Lucky for me, as it happens, that the rains came early and my good friend Eli there, trundled his old prairie schooner into shelter close by.' Will paused a moment. 'But not so lucky for you, eh, Johnny? No, not so lucky at all. You left me for dead back there and sold up my outfit. But I lived, didn't I, made it through to hit the trail again and come to hauntin' you? How'd you like that, Johnny? You ain't gettin' jumpy, are yuh?'

'You're crazed,' dribbled Twist, his gun hand shifting on a shake. 'Mad. You hear that, whoever yuh are?' The sweat beaded like fresh rain on his brow. 'Know what they do with mad dogs? Well, I'll show yuh.'

Twist had thrust his Colt forward in anticipation of the blaze his trigger finger would release; his eyes had widened again, round and shining on the night, his lips shaped to a smirk, but that was as far as his attempt to shoot Will Petty ever got.

The roar from the shadows threw the gunman back into the brush as if a sudden wind had rushed at some loose growth. Seconds later Johnny Twist lay dead.

The silence slipped back and might have settled had it not been for the groan from deep in the darkness of the tumbledown shack.

THIRTEEN

Doc Marley had slept his usual four hours of sound, unbroken sleep through a hot, airless night, and woken in his bed in the small back room to a noise he could not place.

It might, of course, have been one of the scavenging town dogs out on an early prowl. It might have been a stirring drunk homeward bound – save that drunks never made a careful noise such as this had been – or it might, he acknowledged with a tired grunt as he rose from the bed, have been no more than the leftovers of a bad dream.

Save that Doc Marley rarely dreamed.

His first thought in his half-awake state was that the noise had been made by somebody trying to rouse him for his medical services – seeing as how folks' ills always worsened in the small hours. Not so, he decided, opening the front door to the silent street just wide enough to establish there was no one there.

His second thought, and a sight more troubling, was that somebody was trying to break in at the back.

He had crossed quickly to the drawer in his desk where he housed his old Colt and felt a deal safer when it was tight in his grip, then, resisting the instinct to light a lantern, had padded softly through the gloom to the rear of the house.

All quiet now, but that was not to say. . . . The soft scuff of a horse's hoof in the dirt; the merest jangle of tack. The hushed murmur of voices. A step, moving closer. . . .

Doc had waited another ten seconds before strengthening his grip on the Colt and slipping the bolt on the door.

'Thank God!' said a voice from the slowly thinning darkness. 'Sorry to bother you, Doc, but we got some real trouble here.'

And for the second time in a few short hours, Doc Marley stared into the face of the only half-conscious woman.

'Grace Keene, eh?' murmured Doc Marley, through the quiet of the back room in his clapboard home. 'I heard tell of her. Big attraction in Miriam. Had the fellas eatin' out of her hand at the saloon there.'

He sighed, adjusted his spectacles and bent closer to the body on the bed. 'No big attraction now, is she? In a poor way for sure, but you fellas did the right thing in bringin' her in. Probably saved her life. Another day without proper attention and rest and it would have been all over for her.'

The woman moaned, stirred and winced on some deep, inner pain. 'Easy, easy,' soothed Doc, laying a hand on

Grace's brow. 'Lord above knows how she ever got into all this mess – mebbe you can tell me – but I sure as July know I ain't lettin' her outa my sight again. Not for nothin' nor nobody. She's stayin' right here, under my roof. I got some good friends. We'll keep her outa sight and look to her, don't nobody doubt that.'

He turned from the bed to face the two men waiting and watching at the open door. 'Yuh say you shot that fella Johnny Twist? Well, take my advice and clear this town fast as you can before the scum's partners get to checkin' on that shack come sun-up in a couple of hours from now.'

'We ain't ridin' no place,' said Will flatly, his gaze steady and bright in the half light. 'We got some business needs lookin' to.'

'It's a long story, Doc,' added Eli hurriedly, on a weakening grin. 'Goes back some for my friend, Mr Petty, here, but I guess it won't take long to finish once. . . .' He spread his arms. 'What the hell, just glad we saw your board on the door there soon as we did and roused you without bringin' half the town down on our heads.' The grin hovered again. 'Miss Keene there was our only concern o' course. Grateful to you for what you're doin'.' He paused a moment, turning his floppy hat through his hands. 'Don't suppose you'd know why Twist and his friends rode into Kearney, would you?'

'No idea,' answered Doc brusquely, 'save that it wouldn't be for any lawful reason, you can bet your life. Never is with types like them. Either runnin' from trouble or into more of it. We get 'em all the time.' He peered over the top of his spectacles. 'Why? That rat-bag trio happen to be your business, Mr Petty? That why you don't seem too fussed about the shootin' of Twist and ain't ridin' out? And just where does Miss Keene figure in all this? Care to tell me?'

'Johnny dead and the woman gone – well ain't that just apple-pie-dandy!' sneered Stiffkey, scuffing the toe of his boot through the brush and scrub. 'All we need now is for that gold shipment out of Silvertown to be cancelled and we could have ourselves a wake!' He spat fiercely and kicked a loose rock into the undergrowth.

'Ain't no problem with the gold, I guarantee it,' growled Rope Porter moodily, his gaze cold and narrowed on the tumbledown shack. 'Question we got to answer is, who did this? Who shot and killed Johnny and took the woman?'

'And where is he now?' added Stiffkey, spitting again. 'Or mebbe there was more than one of 'em. Mebbe it was a crowd of the townfolk – that nosy Doc and the livery owner. Mebbe we were followed when we brought the woman here in the first place.' He kicked at another rock. 'Pity we had anythin' to do with the bitch. We should've left her with them scum drifters. She was half dead, anyhow. Tell you somethin', Rope, mebbe we should just keep ridin' right now, eh? Keep goin' 'til we hit the border. Forget Kearney, forget the gold. Go raid ourselves a homestead some place, or some lone wagon. That's more our style.'

'We ain't forgettin' the gold, and we ain't leavin' Kearney. We owe it to Johnny to hit the bank and to find his killer,' said Porter, still staring at the shack.

'Very touchin', I'm sure,' clipped Stiffkey, relaxing his

weight to one hip. 'So what yuh suggestin': that we bury the Kid here decent, head back to Kearney, lift the gold from the bank, then go find Johnny's killer?'

'Just that.'

'As easy as hittin' a spittoon at two paces, eh?' mocked Stiffkey. 'I don't think! If whoever shot Johnny and took the woman is back in Kearney right now – and it's my bettin' he is – he's waitin' on us. No question. Sittin' there, satisfied and smilin', just watchin' for us ridin' in. And when we do —'

'If you ain't for it, you can pull out,' said Porter flatly. 'I ain't holdin' yuh to nothin'.'

Stiffkey shrugged, spat and looked for a rock to kick.

Porter's thoughts strayed to Blake Winter and how long it would be before he reached Kearney.

Sheriff Crabbe stared at the as yet unopened bottle of whiskey on his desk, then at the clock on the wall of his office, the window to the street where the slow morning light was breaking like the lift of the lid on a lazy eye, and grunted in response to his jumbled thoughts.

It might be early, he reasoned, but so what the hell? These were difficult times, he had a lot to reckon on; he was shouldering big responsibilities. And doing it alone.

He grunted again, licked his lips, blinked on the sweat round his eyes, and reached for the glass at the side of the bottle. One measure would settle his nerves, soothe his aching stomach, clear his vision for the day ahead. Hell, wearing the badge in Kearney was getting to be just that – a hell. Sooner he was out of it and shaking off the town dust the better. Meantime. . . .

There was Porter, the gold, the planned raid on the bank – and that woman. He swallowed the measure in one gulp and poured another to the empty glass. She was beginning to haunt him, twist and turn in his every thought; there was something about the way she had arrived in Kearney and disappeared again to wherever she was being held that was troubling him sorely.

Why had Porter and his boys gone to so much trouble to grab her from the drifters? What made her of such value to them? How much baggage was she really trailing? And just where might she figure in the coming bank raid?

Sheriff Crabbe had swallowed his second measure of whiskey and was contemplating a third when he moved to the window at the sound of soft hoofs through the street dirt.

Handful of riders, travelled some distance by the look of them; a frock-coated, fancy shirt fellow glancing anxiously round him; rider at his side a deal more relaxed, man of authority – a sheriff, damn it! Could see his badge from here.

Now what was about to be added to his worries, he groaned, pouring a third measure almost without noticing?

FOURTEEN

'Horse-thieves?' frowned Sheriff Crabbe, drumming his fingers absently on his stained, cluttered desk. 'Get most scum through town best part of the time, but I ain't occasioned on horse-thieves in months.' He grimaced and shrugged. 'And yuh say one of 'em's a woman?'

Blake Winter dusted the lapels of his coat. 'Grace Keene – extremely good-lookin', cut above your average bar whore – you might have heard of her. Even in Kearney.'

Crabbe disregarded the sarcasm and shrugged again, his thoughts already working on the image of the woman the trail drifters had brought in. 'Plenty of women hereabouts, but I wouldn't rate any one of 'em as bein' in the class of horse-thief.'

'And no sightin' of any fellas who might be Will Petty and his travellin' partner, Eli Cornpaw?' said Sheriff Cole from where he lounged at the side of the office window.

'Nothin' reckonin' to the description you've given me,' answered Crabbe. 'If them and the woman had arrived together, you can bet I'd have known to it, 'specially if the woman's as good-lookin' as you say.'

Winter picked purposefully at a stray thread on his shirt. 'Strangers in town?' he grinned lightly. 'Had many through these past days?'

'Mister, we got so many strangers in this town, you're hard pushed to find a resident!' scoffed Crabbe, leaning back in his chair, his fingers steepling under his stubbled chin. 'Only strangers who interest me are them totin' fast iron with a hankerin' for provin' the point. They either get thrown out or, when I've the time and a mind, hanged. I ain't fussed either way. As it happens we ain't done any throwin' out or hangin' in weeks. But don't fret, we'll get to it sooner or later!'

The saloon-keeper's grin hovered. 'I'm sure you will, Sheriff. Quite sure. So if I were to ask if the likes of Rope Porter and his sidekicks, Stiffkey and Johnny Twist, are in town, you'd know?'

'Sure I would – and they are. Been here some time, and they ain't causin' no bother. Just passin' through at their leisure.' Crabbe's gaze shifted to Sheriff Cole. 'Don't tell me they're tied in with your horse-thieves?' he frowned.

'Not in this instance,' murmured Cole. 'But they were in Miriam a while back and there was talk —'

'Yes, well,' smiled Winter, settling his coat with a tug, 'towns get to bein' nests of rumours when reputations ride in, don't they? Sheriff Crabbe here knows that well enough. Could spend all day, every day, chasin' rumours, I'll bet. Ain't that so, Sheriff?'

'True enough,' nodded Crabbe on a dry throat as he came to his feet.

'So we'll leave you to the good work for now,' smiled

Winter again. 'Guess we'll be around for a day or so while we give our boys a break and rest the horses. Meantime, if you should happen to see or hear anythin' of our horse-thieves, Mr Cole would appreciate your tellin' him, I'm sure.'

'You bet,' added Cole.

Crabbe had retrieved the bottle of whiskey and the glass from the drawer in his desk within minutes of his early morning visitors heading back to the street.

He did not trust a man like Blake Winter; he was too smooth, too easy, but shifty with it. And horse-thieves, he reckoned, pouring himself his fourth measure, were the least of the fellow's concerns.

'Didn't waste no time, did they?' Eli smacked his lips, narrowed the line of his squint through the gap in the drapes at Doc Marley's front parlour window, and scowled. 'Looks to me as if Sheriff Cole and that dude saloon-keeper have raised a posse out there. Hell, Grace Keene mean that much to them?'

Will Petty grunted and turned from the window to face Doc. 'You reckonin' on bein' able to keep the lady hidden here, out of sight for as long as is needed? Them fellas who've just ridden in ain't goin' to be for showin' a deal of patience when it comes to findin' Miss Keene, 'specially Blake Winter.'

'Leave the woman to me, mister,' said Doc, closing the back bedroom door on the softest click of the latch. 'I got my ways and I got my means. Strikes me as bein' more to the point in gettin' yourselves out of sight. What yuh plannin'? Goin' to be difficult stayin' hidden here in town, unless, o'course, you're plannin' on pullin' out completely. But after the story you've just told me about what happened to yuh, I don't figure for that – not while Rope Porter is around, though I wouldn't give a spit to a fly for his temper when he gets back from seein' what's happened to Johnny Twist.'

'We'll head for that old shack,' announced Will, glancing quickly at Eli. 'Last place anybody'll come lookin' for us. And remember, chances are neither Porter nor Stiffkey are likely to recall my face on a first sight, and they ain't never seen Eli here. That gives us an edge.'

'Paper thin,' croaked Eli, still watching at the window. 'But we don't want to seem greedy!' He covered the gap in the drapes. 'Winter looks as if he's goin' to be holed-up at the saloon there for a while so let's move, eh? Give ourselves some breathin' space.'

Minutes later, they had shaken Doc's hand, murmured their thanks again and slipped away to their mounts through the back door without another sound. Doc watched them fade into the morning shadows, shook his head thoughtfully and figured it would be no bad thing if he kept that old Colt of his to hand.

He had a feeling he might be needing it.

'They're in there – Sheriff Cole, Blake Winter, sidekicks makin' up the posse. Takin' it easy, drinkin', eatin'. Don't look to be in no hurry to leave. So what do you reckon? And more to the point, what we goin' to do about 'em? One sheriff we can handle – and have – but two could get to bein' messy.' Stiffkey wiped the sleeve of his shirt across his sweat-stained face and drew Rope Porter a step deeper into the shadows at the rear of the Gold Rush saloon.

'They ain't got the woman,' muttered Porter vaguely, as if to himself. 'And if they didn't find Grace Keene, they didn't kill Johnny. So who the devil did?'

'Don't know,' snapped Stiffkey impatiently, 'and frankly I ain't much bothered right now. I'm a whole lot more concerned about Sheriff Cole bein' here. How long is he plannin' on stayin' in town? What does Crabbe figure?' He spat fiercely across the dirt. 'You want I should go take care of Cole? Wouldn't be difficult.'

'Killin' a lawman, specially a visitin' lawman, ain't goin' to serve no purpose,' said Porter. 'No,' he added after a pause, 'we wait for the gold to arrive. Shipment's due tomorrow. Then we make our move. Not before.'

'Might be too late,' grunted Stiffkey. 'Yuh might live to regret that decision. Or die on it.'

Porter stayed silent for a moment, his gaze narrowed on the shadows, his thoughts teeming through the recollections of the drunken night with Blake Winter. If there was anyone he needed out of the way, it was the owner of the Dollar Bit.

'Of course,' he murmured, 'who the hell's goin' to miss Blake Winter? Him out of the way would be one less to trouble us.'

Stiffkey twitched and grinned. 'Now you're talkin' like the Rope Porter I ride along of! And you're right, Winter ain't nobody particular, and, who knows, he might have passed that old shack last night; he could've found the woman; could have her hidden away some place – so he might have shot the Kid. That what you're tellin' me, Rope?'

'Yeah, somethin' like that,' murmured Porter again, still watching the shadows.

A half of Sheriff Otis Crabbe's newly opened bottle of whiskey had gone long before mid-afternoon, and its consumption, he had to admit, had done little to solve his problems.

Cole, Blake Winter, their unlikely tale of horse-thieving and a more than passing interest in Rope Porter and the strangers in town. . . . And now, damn it, the shooting by somebody, unknown and unseen, of Johnny Twist and the disappearance of that woman again. Was it surprising, he asked himself, that he had attacked the whiskey?

But the hours were ticking away, he mused, glancing at the clock on the office wall, and the arrival of the Silvertown gold getting closer. Another night, another dawn, and it would be here, securely locked in the safes of the Kearney town bank.

He leaned back in his chair at the desk, eyed the half-empty bottle and the stained glass at its side, and smiled.

He had really nothing to lose, he thought, and now the share-out from the raid would be even higher with Johnny Twist dead. All he really had to do was figure how to keep Sheriff Cole and Blake Winter out of his hair. Perhaps permanently.

He reached for the glass and the half-empty bottle.

FIFTEEN

Sheriff Cole stretched his legs, yawned on a stifled hiss, scratched the back of his head before adjusting his hat, and came to his feet. He glanced lazily round the near deserted, dimly lit saloon bar, yawned again and nodded to his dozing deputies.

'Get m'self a breath of air,' he said, leaving the table in the direction of the batwings. 'Let me know when Winter decides to show his face.' The deputies grunted but stayed dozing.

Cole paused on the boardwalk, looked to left and right, hitched his pants and for no particular reason headed towards the livery where the soft glow from the smoking forge stared like an eye into the evening dusk.

This was the hour when Kearney slept; the waiting time between the heat of the afternoon and the promise of the cooler night, when the bar girls rested, the drunks only half stirred and the silence was broken by no more than the buzz of a fidgety fly.

Cole moved easily, quietly along the boardwalks, pausing occasionally for a closer look at a window, the sign on

96

a door, then to cross the narrow alleys between blocks of buildings where the shadows were already massing for night.

He met few folk at that hour and might have reached Bart Parnham's livery with no more than a murmured greeting, a polite nod to the handful of passers-by had it not been for the sound of a voice he recognized.

He halted abruptly at the steps to the dirt and dust alley and melted into the darker shadow at the door of a one-time tailor's. The voice, somewhere deep in the darkness of the alley, droned on, urgent and incisive as if drilling home a telling point.

Blake Winter out here, pondered Cole, straining to catch at the words? Who had he met? Why? And why there in the shadows? Last he had seen of the saloon-keeper he had been heading in search of one of the better-looking bar girls.

Cole shifted, this time cat-like down the boardwalk steps – praying that they were nailed tight – and drifted into the alley, his back to the building, his eyes glinting, wide and watchful.

The voice tightened, lifted, the words beginning to sharpen and form. Cole stiffened, his concentration intense as the voice rose, fell, became muffled, then cleared.

'. . . so it seems I ain't goin' to be left with a deal of choice, does it?'

The voice of Rope Porter, thought Cole, straining again for the next words.

'No choice at all,' replied Winter bluntly. 'But don't see me as a threat, or someone likely to blow your plan out of

spite. I could, of course, and I might, but not if you see me
as a partner, and let's face it, you're goin' to need another
trusted gun now that you've lost Johnny Twist.'

There was a brief, tense moment of silence before
Porter responded.

'Like I say, no choice. Should've kept my mouth shut
back there in Miriam.'

'But that's the past, Rope. This is now and your whole
future's comin' up mighty fast. Do we have a deal?'

Another silence.

'Yuh got it,' grunted Porter. 'But on two conditions.'

'Name 'em.'

'Yuh got a sheriff and his deputies ridin' along of yuh in
some so-called posse trailin' horse-thieves. You get rid of
'em, and fast. Sheriff Crabbe here is with us. He's in on the
raid, and we need him as law-abidin' cover, but he's all the
law we do need. You understand?'

'Understood,' said Winter. 'Leave Cole and his boys to
me. And the second?'

'Second, that woman yuh had workin' for you – Grace
Keene. What we goin' to do about her?'

'Do we need to do anythin' right now?'

Cole shifted his shoulders against a creeping numbness
and peered hard into the curtain of darkness that had
seemed to thicken in minutes.

A boot scuffed at dirt, and then Porter spoke again.
'Somebody shot Johnny Twist at the shack. That same
somebody took the woman. Who is that somebody, and
where is he now?'

Cole could picture the cold glint in Porter's eyes.

'Hell, how should I know?' said Winter. 'Sorry about

Johnny, of course, sure I am, but the woman ain't nothin' compared along of the gold. We'll get to her once we've made the raid. She can't have gotten far. Damn it, she might be right here in town even now. She rode out of Miriam with a fella name of Will Petty. He's the one we need to find. He'll know about her.'

'Never heard of nobody goin' by the name of Petty,' snapped Porter. 'Who's he?'

'Don't matter none. Him and the woman is somethin' else you can leave to me. All you and Stiffkey gotta do from here on is —'

A trickle of icy sweat in Sheriff Cole's neck had forced him to twitch, hunch his shoulders and raise a hand instinctively to the irritation. It was enough to disturb the shape of the shadows and for Winter's head to turn sharply to the unseen movement, his glare as sharp and penetrating as steel.

'Who the hell's there?' grunted Porter, drawing his Colt through a smooth flash of fingers.

Cole pressed himself tighter to the clapboard as if hoping it might swallow him. Blake Winter drew his bone-handled Colt and probed it menacingly into the darkness.

'Don't move a whisker whoever yuh are,' growled Porter, stepping to the centre of the alley, his stance straddled, gun firm and steady.

Cole licked his lips, felt the sweat wet on his back, looked anxiously to the main street and the smudges of lantern light at a handful of windows. Too late now to make a dash for them, he decided. He would be lucky to take a half-dozen steps before Porter's gun blazed. He licked his lips again, relaxed his fingers and began slowly to raise his arms clear of his holster in surrender. Nothing else for it, but somebody was in for a big surprise once he saw the face in the shadows.

'See now why you were so keen to ride for Kearney,' said Cole, his back to the street, arms raised, his gaze flat and unblinking on the taut, ashen face of Blake Winter. 'But hell, I never figured for you grovelling this low.' He spat harshly into the dirt. 'If you're reckonin' on gettin' away with this, you'd best think again. Yuh got about as much chance as a fly in honey.'

'That's enough of the lip, Sheriff,' sneered Porter, tightening his grip on the probing Colt. 'Fella here knows what he's about, and that ain't none of your business. Your problem is bein' here. Yuh see that, don't yuh? Yuh know clear enough where this is headin'?'

'Even you wouldn't have the guts to take me out,' croaked Cole, beginning to twitch, the sweat on his brow glistening.

'Mebbe we should —'

'This is my show,' growled Porter, 'and I ain't for havin' it messed by no nosy-parkerin' lawman, 'specially one out of a two-bits town like Miriam. You made a bad decision in ridin' for Kearney. Real bad. Shame.'

It was the speed then, the merciless rage of Porter's gun through three fast shots throwing Cole to the dirt, that froze Blake Winter where he stood, his eyes round, wide and white, his mouth suddenly dry as the dust on his boots and the soft curl of smoke through the alley.

'Hell,' murmured Winter, 'did yuh have to? Was that really necessary? I could have. . . . We're goin' to have half the town here in about ten seconds flat.'

Porter stared at the sprawled body of the sheriff for a moment, holstered his gun and narrowed his cold, hawk-ish gaze on the street ahead. 'Didn't see the fella properly. Mistook him in the dark for some stinkin' drifter waitin' here to jump us. . . . Happens all the time in Kearney. That's the story. We stick with it.' He spat and grinned. 'Don't worry about Crabbe. He'll see things our way. He ain't got no choice.'

Winter stifled a shiver across his back, his gaze still on the body and the thickening stains of blood. 'What about Cole's deputies, the fellas in the posse?'

'Tell 'em to get back to Miriam and wait on news from the territorial marshal. They'll ride, sure enough. They won't be for hangin' on here.' Porter glared quickly at the saloon-keeper. 'And get a grip on yourself, f'Cris'sake. This body ain't goin' to be the last you'll see. We're only just gettin' started.'

SIXTEEN

Doc Marley had heard the three shots and been struggling into his frock-coat, rummaging through the shadowy gloom and clutter of his front parlour for his bag for a full minute before the call came for him to 'Get the hell here fast, Doc, we got a body!'

Otis Crabbe, Rope Porter, Blake Winter and a gathering of neck-craning, muttering onlookers were waiting for him in the alley, their shadows reaching across the lifeless body like tombstones.

'Real tragedy we got ourselves here,' began Crabbe, eyeing Doc with a respectful if brief sidelong glance. 'Seems like Mr Porter mistook the fella for some no-good drifter lurkin' back here, doubtless waitin' on an easy-pickin' for his next drink, and before he knew what had happened —'

'He'd shot him,' concluded Doc bluntly, examining the body. 'I can well imagine,' he added in a dry, wry tone. 'Happens all the time around Kearney, don't it? Any day, any night. Place wouldn't be the same without a dead body to decorate it – 'ceptin' that dead sheriffs ain't exactly a regular occurrence.'

He stood fully upright, straightened the pleats of his coat and stared over the rims of his spectacles at Crabbe. 'You aware this fella is a lawman, Sheriff? You also aware of the implications of the shootin' of such a person – accidental or otherwise, it don't matter which – and that Territorial Marshal Haskett must be informed and will sure as hell want some sort of inquiry?'

'Yes, yes,' gestured Crabbe, irritably, glancing anxiously at the growing crowd of onlookers. 'Yuh don't have to remind me. I'll handle it. Meantime, let's get to it, eh, Doc, and clear the street? This fella dead by shootin'?'

'Very dead,' grunted Doc. 'Shot three times, close range.'

'That's good enough,' pronounced Crabbe. 'Now somebody go get the undertaker.'

Doc had half turned for a quiet word in livery owner Bart Parnham's ear when he paused mid-breath and narrowed his gaze on the figure slipping silently back to the deeper shadows. Unless he had been a whole heap mistaken that had been Will Petty taking a more than close interest in the activities in the alley.

Doc grunted quietly to himself and laid a hand on Bart's shoulder. 'My place, five minutes,' he murmured. 'We got things to discuss.'

'If this town ain't a powder-keg, I ain't Bart Parnham, and that's the fact of it.' The livery owner mopped feverishly at his brow with a large polka-dot bandanna and blinked on the clouding sweat. 'That's a full-fledged, sworn sheriff goin' corpse-cold out there. Shot here, in our town, under our very noses by another of those scumbag gunslingers we seem to attract like flies. And did you see Crabbe; did you see the look on his face? Couldn't give a damn to a spittoon, could he?'

Bart mopped again, pocketed the bandanna and accepted the glass of whiskey poured for him by Doc Marley. 'Your health, Doc,' he murmured, gulping on the measure. 'Sure as hell in need of this – a whole bottle of it way things are goin'!'

Doc sighed, took a gulp of his own drink and went softly to the part closed door to the back room, listened for a moment, then eased away on a satisfied grunt. 'Woman's sleepin' like a babe,' he said quietly. 'Which is just what she needs.'

Bart crossed to the window of the parlour and stared into the night-shadowed street. 'But she's goin' to be a problem, you can bet to it. How long do you figure on keepin' her hidden like that? From what you've said, it wouldn't surprise me if she ain't the reason why the gunslingers are gatherin' thick as hornets. And if, as you tell me, Will Petty is here, hell-bent on retribution. . . . Don't bear thinking to, does it?'

Doc tapped a finger on the side of his glass. 'No,' he reflected, thoughtfully, 'Grace Keene ain't the whole reason for what's happenin' I'm certain of that. There's gotta be somethin' else; somethin' big enough, important enough, or mebbe. . . .' He paused, the finger unmoving on the glass. 'Lucrative enough —'

'Now that's where you just might have somethin', Doc,' said Bart, turning from the window. 'Lucrative. . . .' He repeated the word as if walking round it. 'Money, or better still gold.' He placed his empty glass on the parlour table.

'I heard 'em sayin' at the bank as how there's a hefty shipment due here out of Silvertown sometime this week. It could be —'

'That Porter and his sidekicks are involved,' added Doc. 'And it could be that Blake Winter fella's tied in some place. In fact, it could be it all began back there in Miriam.'

He poured another measure of whiskey into Bart's glass. 'You're right we're goin' to need this.'

'I should kill yuh, right here, right now. Yuh know that?' Stiffkey stared into Rope Porter's eyes without blinking. 'About all you're good for from where I'm standin'.'

Porter relaxed in the chair in the gloomily lit hotel room, stared back at his partner and smiled softly. 'Yuh would to, savin' for the prospect of gettin' your hands on that gold.'

'If there's goin' to be any gold! Damnit, the way you seem to have been tellin' everybody about the raid we got planned, we'll be lucky if there's enough in the share-out for a measure of sourmash!' His stare iced over. 'Why'd yuh have to go spillin' the plan to Winter? Drunk, I suppose. You bet. And now yuh got yourself into the shootin' of a lawman. Say this for yuh, Rope, you sure ride the dark side of a dirty trail when yuh put your mind to it!'

'Winter was a mistake, I grant you that,' gestured Porter, 'but he ain't goin' to be of no consequence. I'll personally see to that.'

'Meanin'?'

'Meanin' I'll finish him long before he gets his fancy hands anywhere near the gold – *our* gold. Yours and mine.'

'And the dead sheriff? What about him?'

Porter stretched his legs. 'Crabbe'll take care of that, and we'll be all through with Kearney before any marshal starts pokin' about. And mebbe we'll take care of Crabbe if it becomes necessary. So you see —'

'I see nothin' to my likin',' snapped Stiffkey, his stare flashing on a blink. 'You ain't said nothin' as to who shot Johnny and took the woman. Johnny's killer could be here now, down there, somewhere in the street, or mebbe havin' himself a quiet beer at the bar. And as for that woman —'

'I shall make a present of her to you, my friend,' grinned Porter. 'And that's a promise.'

And promises out of Rope Porter's mouth were about as welcome as a rattler's venom, thought Stiffkey.

Sheriff Crabbe glanced furtively at the two stiff measures still left in the bottle of whiskey on his desk. They were going to stay there until this whole business was through, he had decided. Not another drop would pass his lips, and when it did it would be to toast his new life and wealth.

Meantime, he was sweating and getting nervy.

The planned bank raid was becoming messy. It was bad enough having the shooting of a lawman to handle and cover up; it was adding salt to the wound to be told by Porter that the fancy tailored saloon owner, Blake Winter, had joined the raiders. Well, considered Crabbe, maybe he had at that and maybe he would have to be accommodated.

But only for now.

There might come a moment – there most certainly

would come a moment – when Winter's share of the heist would have to be redistributed. After all, who was fronting the preparations for the raid; who would be in the front line of activities from the minute the gold shipment arrived in town?

It would be only one man's responsibility to oversee the shipment into safety. And that man, Sheriff Otis Crabbe, would be stone-cold sober till it was done. And then suitably rewarded for his trouble. You bet!

He grunted, tucked his shirt into his pants, adjusted his gun belt and settled his hat on his head. He would take a last stroll round town, check that all was quiet and as it should be. Tomorrow was going to be a busy day and he wanted the shipment to arrive to a peaceful, easy-going, uncluttered town. No mess, not until it became inevitable.

Meantime, he was still sweating and still nervy.

SEVENTEEN

It was close to noon on another hot, cloudless day when the gold shipment wagon, complete with its guard of a half-dozen heavily armed outriders, pulled into town and was reined to a halt outside the bank.

It took exactly thirty organized minutes – as timed on the saloon bar clock by Rope Porter – for the gold to be unloaded and manhandled into the safety of the bank under the watchful supervision of Sheriff Crabbe.

A further hour passed before the wagon team and the men had been rested and refreshed and were ready to make the return journey to Silvertown. Only then were the doors to the bank finally bolted for the day while the manager, J. J. Setters, assessed the true value of the new deposit and discussed its security in detail with Crabbe.

It was early evening when the lawman left the bank by the back door and hurried to a meeting with Porter, Stiffkey and Blake Winter with the news of a change of plan.

'We're goin' to have to make the hit sooner than we reckoned,' he had clipped bluntly, once into Porter's hotel room.

'How much sooner?' Winter had asked, his colour already beginning to pale.

'Tomorrow.'

'Hell!' Stiffkey had cursed. 'What's the hurry f'Cris'sake?'

'Setters has heard as how some big company back East wants the gold shipped on immediately. Their men are already headin' for Kearney. Could be here any time, so we're goin' to have to shift.'

Winter had picked nervously at the lapels of his coat. 'But we ain't ready, are we?' he had croaked.

'Goin' to have to be.' Porter had poured a long measure of whiskey. 'We ain't waited this long to ride out empty-handed. 'Sides, we owe it to Johnny. We'll hit the place first light t'morrow. Fast, accurate, no messin'. All through and clearin' town in no more than minutes. It can be done. Goin' to have to be done. We agreed?'

'But what about —' Winter had begun.

'We still got unfinished business hereabouts,' Stiffkey had growled. 'Johnny's killer for one. That woman, Grace Keene, for another.'

Porter had thudded his empty glass to the table. 'The only business concernin' me right now is the business of gold and gettin' it out of that bank. Ain't nothin' and nobody else counts a spit. And that's how we all got to see it. Now let's get to the plannin'. We ain't got time enough to be wastin' it.'

Stiffkey had sniffed and grunted. Crabbe helped himself to a measure of Porter's whiskey. Blake Winter had simply paled to a sickly grey.

*

'We're puttin' our necks right on the line here, you realize that, don't yuh?' Eli muttered thoughtfully as he moved like a shadow at Will Petty's side. 'Somebody's certain to see us, and you can bet your sweet life to a pouch of old baccy it'll be somebody who recognizes us.'

Will hushed the old man, laid a hand on his arm and drew him into the deeper darkness in the clutter at the rear of the saloon.

'What yuh see?' croaked Eli, blinking on the gloom. 'You spotted somebody? Somebody out there! Damn it, it's like tryin' to see. . . . Hold it, I got it. Somebody behind that door top of the steps?'

Will grunted and fixed his gaze on the stairway.

'Somebody figurin for makin' a move when he's sure the coast is clear,' hissed Eli. 'He's bein' real careful. Ain't for bein' spotted if he's got half the chance. You don't suppose —'

The door creaked open. A shaft of soft lantern light spread to the steps. Shadows melted, new shapes took their place. A figure eased to the first step and waited.

'Stiffkey?' murmured Eli, straining to probe the darkness. 'Porter's sidekick? Where the hell's he goin'?'

'Give him a start and we'll follow,' said Will.

'Might've guessed you'd figure for that.' The old man adjusted his hat with a flourish. 'Mebbe we should've stayed back there at the shack,' he hissed. 'Saved all this 'til daylight. Give ourselves a half decent chance, 'stead of. . . . There he goes. Ain't wastin' no time, neither.'

'The livery, that's where he's headed,' said Will.

'Don't tell me he's for pullin' out.'

'Not with all that gold we seen bein' shipped in takin'

up space in the bank,' quipped Will. 'Prospect of that's goin' to make bushwhackin' look a mite tame. Well, we'll see. Let's move. Stay back, but keep the rat in your sight.'

'You ain't —'

But by then they were moving and Eli's words were lost.

Stiffkey slid quickly, silently through the shadows at the rear of the main street buildings, his steps heading steadily for the livery stables. He paused only once to look back to the saloon as if to reassure himself he was still alone, then moved again unaware of the shadows to his left and the figures moving through them.

'Get round to the front of the place,' murmured Will. 'Keep watch from the street. Leave this side to me.'

Eli grunted and narrowed his gaze. 'Got yuh. But you just go easy, yuh hear! Just 'cos I ain't at your side to look to you don't mean to say —'

Will slapped the old man's shoulders. 'Shift,' he insisted. 'Don't let's get to losin' this scumbag.'

Eli grunted again, pushed at his floppy hat and disappeared to leave Will with his concentration still focused on Stiffkey as he continued to make his way to the stables.

He followed, always at a distance, always in the shadows, his gaze tight and unmoving on the gunslinger's back. Not until Stiffkey had moved carefully into the darkness of the stabling did he increase his pace to close quickly on the open frontage, pause a moment, watch, listen, tap the butt of his holstered Colt, and then slip like something on a breeze into the silence.

He was aware instantly of the tone of Stiffkey's low, incisive voice. 'You Bart Parnham, owner of this two-bit outfit?'

Bart spluttered indignantly from behind the soft glow

of a low lit lantern. 'As a matter of fact, I am, and I'll
thank you —'

'The same fella I seen comin' out of the doc's place?'

'That don't seem to me to be no business of yours.'

'Yes or no?' snapped Stiffkey.

'It so happens Doc Marley is a personal friend of mine,'
said Bart importantly. 'A *close* friend. Him and me, we go
back some and between us manage to keep this town just
short of slippin' —'

'As I thought,' clipped Stiffkey. 'In other words, you
and that doc between you would know just about most
things goin' on in Kearney. Right?'

'You could say that.'

'So if I mentioned the name, Grace Keene, you'd know
who I was talkin' about?'

'I don't know no such person,' blustered Bart. 'I ain't
never heard —'

'She holed up at Doc's place?' persisted Stiffkey. 'That
where you're hidin' her?'

'I don't know who you are, mister, but I sure as hell —'

Stiffkey spat noisily across the floor. 'Me and my partners took the woman out of them trail-drifters' grubby
paws and were holdin' her safe at a disused shack far side
of town, 'til some sharp-shootin' stranger seems to have
stepped in and not only moved the woman on some place,
but shot Johnny Twist into the bargain. And that, fella, I
do not like, not no how I don't.'

The gunslinger eased his weight to one hip. 'Now,
seems to me that whoever took the lady wouldn't have
been unaware of her condition and figure for her needin'
a doc pretty smartish. Right? You followin' me here, Mr

Livery-man? Good. So. . . . What better than the doc right here in Kearney? Seems kinda logical, don't it?'

Bart shifted uneasily in the lantern glow, his eyes flicking in their sockets like fish.

'That why you been in and out of Doc Marley's place so much this past day? I've been notin' how busy you've been. You been helpin' the doc? Checkin' on the woman?'

Bart began to sweat. 'I still don't know who or what you're talkin' about. I ain't never seen or heard —'

'We goin' to do this the easy way, or is it goin' to get messy?' grinned Stiffkey. 'I could whip it out of you, o'course, but it'd be a whole lot better it you came straight out with it. T'ain't no big deal for yuh. I mean, all I want is to take good care of the lady.' The grin faded, his eyes gleamed. 'Now, is the woman holed-up at doc's place? Three seconds, that's all yuh got.'

'Save your breath.'

Bart gulped and shuddered under his lathering of sweat at the cold steel of the voice from somewhere in the shadows.

Stiffkey spun round, a hand instinctively on the butt of his holstered Colt. 'Who the hell's there?' he croaked, his eyes like glowing lights.

The shadows danced for a moment in the flickering of the lantern glow.

'Who are yuh?' hissed Stiffkey, the eyes narrowing for the glimpse of a shape. 'Step out where I can see you before they have to carry you out. And do it now, mister. Right now!'

'Last time you invited me to step anywhere was from my wagon,' said Will without moving. 'Didn't work too well for me then. Three against one, as I recall, and you weren't none too easy with the bull-whip you were handlin' that day.'

'What the hell you talkin' about, mister?' growled Stiffkey, his fingers twitching on the gun butt, eyes straining for the slightest movement.

'Will somebody —' shivered Bart, but swallowed his words on a searing growl and glare from Stiffkey.

'You stay right where you are, Mr Livery-man, and don't shift so much as a finger if you know what's good for you,' snapped the gunslinger, his gaze settling again on the darkness. 'And as for you, whoever yuh are, skulkin' there in the shadows, you got just as long as it takes for me to draw this piece before you get to see the far side of oblivion. I hope I make myself creek water clear.'

'Oh, sure,' said Will almost lightly. 'I know all about creeks, seein' as how yuh left me for dead in one. You recall that? Somewhere off the main trail into Miriam. Could take you to the spot blindfold. Oh, yes, I could do that. I can still smell the place. I still got the stench of them who left me there under my nose. Smelled it real strong back at that old trail shack and the sight of your partner, Johnny Twist. I got rid of it then, but now it's back to troublin' me again. . . .'

EIGHTEEN

Stiffkey's Colt blazed on a hiss and growl as the gunslinger crouched low and tight, his eyes as wild as the shots, the sweat beading like ice on his brow. Bart Parnham fell back, darkening the lantern glow for a moment with the bulk of his staggering body.

Timbers splintered under the hail of hot lead; smoke and the smell of cordite slid across the darkness. 'Well, fella,' croaked Stiffkey, 'yuh had a taste there. You want I should make it a real meal for you?'

A nervous horse snorted and stamped in a stall at the far end of the stables; Bart half stifled a moan and shifted noisily.

'You keep still there,' growled Stiffkey, his grip reshaping on the butt of the Colt as he probed it ahead of him like an iron antennae and his eyes narrowed on the misted gloom. 'Don't nobody move – 'specially not you out there, mister. You still with us, or you had second thoughts about tanglin' with me? You want my advice, you'd best hightail it while you're still drawin' breath.'

Silence.

Bart gulped, wondering how long it would be before

the townsfolks' curiosity got the better of them and they came in search of the shootist.

Stiffkey licked at the sweat on his lips. 'I'm waitin', fella,' he drawled. 'Don't you go tryin' my patience now. I ain't a patient man.'

'Just at your lousy best when you're bull-whippin' somebody, eh, and kickin' 'em naked into a dry-bed creek?'

The voice came from the other side of the building where the darkness was thicker, unbroken, hanging like a funeral shroud.

Stiffkey swung round, fired a fast, loose shot, blinked and crouched still lower. 'Rat!' he murmured. 'Skulkin' rat. Why, you ain't nothin' more than vermin.' He spat. 'I'm tellin' you, mister, just this once —'

'No, Stiffkey, you're all through talkin'. You've just got yourself a pressin' appointment – in Hell!'

Will Petty's gun blazed two fast shots. Stiffkey fell back, his gaze wild, curses spitting from him, his fingers squirming like wet worms across a bleeding shoulder wound.

Bart stumbled in his shock and trembling fear, lost his footing and crashed to the floor, threatening for a moment to carry the lantern with him. He scrambled to retrieve it, steadied his grip and watched open-mouthed as the shadow of the groaning Stiffkey shrank like some grotesque hunchback and Will's loomed long and black across the stable walls.

Will kicked aside Stiffkey's Colt and closed on the grovelling gunslinger through slow, measured steps. His gaze tightened; he fired a third shot, watched Stiffkey's eyes take on a focused glaze of part recall, part despair as words began to form but died on the man's last breath.

Will grunted, turned quickly and with barely a glance at the bewildered livery owner disappeared into the darkness.

'Get back! Just get back there, will yuh? There ain't nothin' to see.'

Sheriff Crabbe waved his arms at the crowd of townsmen pressing for a closer look into the lantern-lit stables.

'Who's dead, Sheriff?' called a man at the back of the gathering.

'Is that the fella they call Stiffkey?' echoed another. 'Heard as how he'd been headin' this way.'

'Who the hell did the shootin'?'

'Yeah, who did that? You get him? He still around?'

'Mebbe we should organize a search. What yuh reckon, Sheriff?'

The crowd murmured and pressed forward again.

Crabbe spread his arms. 'Mebbe, mebbe,' he soothed, standing his ground, 'but not now. Not 'til I done a whole lot more investigatin' here and I seen what's what.'

'Ain't much to see that ain't plain enough, is there?' called an old man from the shadows.

'He's right, sure enough. Shootin' is shootin' – straight as that. Where's Bart? What's he got to say?'

'Yeah, and where's Doc? He seen the body?'

'Doc's seen the body and left, Bart's in the forge, and he ain't for bein' disturbed 'til I've had words with him,' said Crabbe defiantly. 'Now, will you all shift your butts and leave me to do my job? Let's go!'

The townsmen murmured among themselves and began to shuffle back to the brighter light of the main

street where the bar girls and not so curious onlookers
waited for news.

'I'm sleepin' with my gun strapped to me t'night,'
grunted a bearded man.

'Same here.'

A third man halted and gestured for the others to come
closer. 'All very well for Crabbe there gettin' high and
mighty with his law-keepin',' he said, lowering his voice,
'but we all seen what he makes of his so-called *investigatin*'.'

'Investigatin' what's in a bottle, more like!' hissed the
old man sarcastically.

'And what about that sheriff shot dead by Porter?'
asked the bearded man. 'We ain't heard a deal more about
that, have we? All Crabbe did was to send them Miriam
deputies ridin' for the marshal. And what about them
dead drifters and the woman they had with 'em? Don't
seem to be a deal of *investigatin*' there.'

The gesturing man's voice lowered again. 'Now listen
up there, all of you. With all that gold sittin' in the bank,
the last thing we need in town is a loose gun. So I've got a
proposition: we leave Crabbe to himself, but meantime we
keep t'gether, all of us; mount our own watch on this town
and who's comin' and goin' through it. What yuh say?'

'I say we do it. Be a whole sight safer all round, 'specially
for the womenfolk.'

The gathering murmured agreement.

'Right, so let's go have ourselves a drink and do some
plannin'. . . .'

'It's gettin' out of hand. Mebbe we should call it off, forget the gold, just get ourselves clear of this town before it swallows us all. I tell you straight up there's somebody watchin' us. Somebody who wants us dead.'

Blake Winter hunched his shoulders against the chill of a shiver and turned his drawn grey face from the faint glow of the lantern-light and stared from the livery stables to the street.

'Yuh been tellin' me an awful lot of late,' said Rope Porter, lifting his gaze from the blood-soaked body of Stiffkey, 'and I've been listenin' to you, Blake. Sure I have. Every goddamn word.' He paused, spat, adjusted his hat and hitched his gunbelt. 'And yuh know what, my friend? You're talkin' rot!'

'But look at the facts, will yuh?' said Winter, turning sharply. 'You've lost Johnny and now Stiffkey, probably – in truth, darned near certainly – to the same gun. Don't that suggest somethin' to yuh, somethin' very like somebody with a real urge to see Rope Porter and his partners six-feet under, by any means, any time, anywhere? Sure as hell does to me.' He pulled dramatically at the lapels of his coat. 'You've lost the woman. Nobody seems to know where she's holed-up. You've been forced to eliminate Sheriff Cole. How long before we have a marshal on our backs? And what about Crabbe? Is he to be trusted? Can we count on him? Hell, the gold's here, sure enough, but just where are we?'

Porter sighed and spat again. 'You for pullin' out, fella?' he asked on a throaty growl. 'You tellin' me I got to do this raid on my own with only Crabbe to count to? That what yuh sayin'? Well, if that's the case, mister, you ride out right now, this very minute, before a grievin' mind finally snaps and I get to takin' out the loss of my good friend, Stiffkey, here, in the only way I know how – by shootin' the first person I'm lookin' at! You get that clear enough?'

'All I'm sayin' is —' began Winter, but swallowed the words as Crabbe emerged from the shadows and joined them.

'Bart Parnham ain't sayin' a deal. Says he didn't recognize the fella who shot Stiffkey. He just appeared, as if he'd been waitin', or followin'.' The sheriff ran a hand round his sweat-sticky neck. 'Stranger in town, gotta be.'

'Did the killer say anythin'?' grunted Porter. 'Damn it, he didn't just stroll in here and blaze away. Don't make sense. Fella must've been killin' for a reason.'

'Same reason he had for shootin' Johnny Twist,' muttered Winter.

'What's this?' frowned Crabbe. 'You sayin' as how there's somebody here in Kearney hell-bent on retribution? I got a blood-blind shootist on my hands?'

'Rot!' growled Porter. 'You ain't got no such thing. You've got some gun-happy kid tryin' to prove himself. We'll get him – tonight if need be.'

'For some kid tryin' to prove himself, he's makin' a pretty good job of it!' sneered Winter, half turning to narrow his eyes on the shadowed street. 'More likely somebody from your past,' he added, images of Will Petty and the shooting at the Dollar Bit crowding his mind. 'Simply waitin'. . . .'

'I didn't tell Crabbe a thing. No description worth the lookin' to, no name, just the bare facts – my version of 'em, anyhow!' Bart Parnham blinked, swallowed his drink

in a single gulp, winced and heaved a sigh of relief.
'Needed that, Doc,' he said, wincing again. 'This rate I'll
be owin' you a whole distillery!' He rolled his shoulders.
'Did I do the right thing?' he asked anxiously.

'Sure you did,' smiled Doc Marley, turning from the
window in his parlour. 'I doubt if our sheriff will be rushin'
round to find Kearney's mysterious killer. I reckon for him
havin' other things on his mind – not least that heap of
gold sittin' in the bank.'

'You figure for Porter bein' here because of the gold?'
said Bart. 'Lost the best part of his guns if he was plannin'
a raid along of Johnny Twist and Stiffkey.'

'There's that fancy dude, Winter, keepin' his close
company.'

'Mebbe, but let me tell you, Doc, Will Petty's in one
helluva mood for settlin' old scores. I heard him back
there in the livery. I saw him, and believe me, that's some
mood he's in.' Bart glanced quickly at the back bedroom
door, then settled a steady gaze on Doc. 'Way I see things
goin' in this town, I'd reckon for us havin' to watch the
woman there like we were hawks. Stiffkey was hell-bent on
findin' her. Mebbe Porter's of a similar mind. Mebbe he'll
come lookin' for her – if he gets the chance.'

Doc listened to the night silence as if expecting it to
creak.

NINETEEN

Blake Winter drew easily on the cigar and let the smoke curl gently through the gloom of the hotel bedroom. His eyes narrowed in their concentration on the street scene beyond the window; the hurried comings and goings; groups of men gathered in the shadows, their conversations tight, their gazes watchful; stamping and snorting of hitched mounts at the saloon; the two men on guard at the bank.

And Bart Parnham glancing nervously around him as he closed the front door of Doc Marley's clapboard home and headed anxiously for the livery.

Winter followed his steps, watched his brusque dismissal of a beckoning wave from the boardwalk, the twitchy half smile to a group gesturing for him to join them, the quickening pace as he reached the deeper shadows at the forge and disappeared.

He blew another curling shaft of cigar smoke, tapped the ash to a bowl on the table at his side, and grunted to the turn of his thoughts. He was sure now he was right: Doc Marley was hiding something, or, more likely, somebody, and he would wager his last dollar that somebody was Grace Keene.

It had to be, he thought, grunting again. It figured. Whoever had shot Johnny Twist at the shack had brought the woman back to town. She had needed medical attention. Doc would have provided it and he was not the type to flinch from offering shelter. And Bart Parnham knew about it, hence his anxious behaviour.

But, he considered through more cigar smoke, if Grace was here in Kearney and holed-up at Doc's place, she was probably the most valuable bargaining piece to hand in the planned bank raid. With Johnny Twist and Stiffkey out of the reckoning when it came to the guns available, the value of Grace Keene as a hostage might be worth a dozen Colts.

He made a final draw on the cigar, watched the smoke cloud the windowpane for a moment then clear like a curtain lifting to the light. He smiled wryly to himself. Somebody had to get a proper grip on the planning of the raid before it was too late. Rope Porter was all recrimination and gun talk; Otis Crabbe all sweat and the smell of liquor. This was no time for slack thinking. They had only hours, very short hours, until the bank opened its doors to the new day's custom – or maybe the arrival in town of the men due to collect the gold. Now was the time to make a move. Do something positive, definite.

He stubbed out the cigar, collected his hat, checked the set of his Colt, and left the room.

Winter went quickly from the hotel to the poorly lit street heading in the direction of Doc Marley's single-storey clapboard home.

He passed the busy saloon with barely a second glance, slid through the boardwalk shadows like a cat, tipped his hat and murmured some apology to a tottering drunk, and smiled thinly at a bar girl sneaking clear of the lights for a breath of clean air.

He had no precise notion of how he was going to handle what he had in mind, save that stepping up to Doc's front door, pulling on the bell cord and waiting for him to answer seemed simple enough and the safest way into his home. Once inside . . . that raised a whole clutter of uncertainties best dealt with as he faced them.

Doc was a while slipping the bolt and opening the door the fraction necessary to recognize his visitor without the aid of a light.

'I ain't in business not unless it's real urgent,' he croaked, blinking over the rims of his spectacles.

'We ain't met, Doc, but I need to see yuh – now,' said Winter, his right boot already poised to slip between the door and the jamb. 'It's important,' he added on a hissed whisper. 'It's concernin' Grace Keene.'

There was a moment of silence. 'Grace Keene?' murmured Doc. 'I don't know no Grace Keene.'

'I think you do, Doc, and if you value her life you'll hear what I got to tell yuh.'

Silence, hesitation.

'Who the hell are you, mister?'

'Blake Winter. Rode in from Miriam with Sheriff Cole's posse.'

'You tied in with that Rope Porter scumbag?'

'I know him, yes. We've talked – and it's because we have that you've got to hear me out. I'm tellin' you, it's urgent.'

The door inched wider. Doc peered closer. 'Three minutes, that's all you've got. I'm busy back here. Town's pilin' up corpses like it was collectin' 'em. Step inside, and make it quick.'

Winter sighed quietly to himself, tapped the butt of his Colt and stepped carefully into Doc's darkened parlour, closing the door softly behind him.

'Kinda dark in here, ain't it?' said Winter.

'Prefer it that way,' snapped Doc, irritably. 'Now, what is it you wanna say? Let's get to it.'

Winter's narrowed eyes pierced the gloom. He noted the position of the furniture, the fully draped window, the ghostly face of the clock, the half-open door to a back room. 'Where you holdin' her?' he clipped.

'What the hell you talkin' about?' began Doc, pushing angrily at his glasses, wondering if he could reach the roll-top desk and grab his Colt without the visitor suspecting.

'She in that room back there? Will Petty and that old-timer bring her in?' clipped Winter again. 'Ain't no point in playin' cat and mouse over this.'

'I'll tell you somethin', mister —'

'And don't even think of movin'. I got a gun trained on yuh here and I won't hesitate to use it. So, I'll put it to yuh again: is Grace Keene back there, or do you want me to go see for myself and drag her out here?'

Doc groaned. 'She's there – but if you so much as lay a finger on her. . . .'

'Now we're gettin' somewhere,' smiled Winter. 'Wise fella. Let's see if you can keep it up.' He stepped to the back-room door and pushed it fully open, the barrel of his Colt glinting on the faintest glimmer of light through the drapes. 'Here's what I want you to do. No arguin', no messin'. You foul up, and the woman here is dead. You understand?'

Doc gulped, removed his spectacles and blinked on the gloom. 'What you sayin'?' he hissed.

'Grace Keene and me go back some. She was in my employ until recently; owes me for most of what she ever was. And she ain't done payin' back!'

Doc gulped again. 'Mebbe she reckons other.'

'Her reckonin' don't figure in it,' scowled Winter, glancing into the room, his grip on the Colt whitening his knuckles. 'Here's what you're goin' to do: you go from here to Sheriff Crabbe's office, find Rope Porter, tell him what's happened, that I'm holdin' the woman and want to see him and Crabbe here. You bring them back. You don't stop for nobody; you don't talk to nobody. I'll be watchin' every step. Slightest thing goes wrong, and I shoot the woman. No messin'. So no heroics, no double dealin'. You got all that?'

'You're goin' to hold Grace Keene hostage,' said Doc, folding his spectacles to their case. 'Against what, f'Cris'sake? Or need I ask? A shipment of gold to the bank here wouldn't be in your reckonin' would it?'

Winter stiffened. 'Just get into your coat and grab your hat, will you? Get movin'!'

'Hope you ain't figurin' on gettin' away with this,' murmured Doc, fumbling into his coat, wishing he was three steps closer to the rolltop desk and his Colt. 'Don't get countin' out your chickens just yet!' he added, as he shuffled to the front door.

*

Eli stepped away from the glow of the light through the saloon batwings and backed into the shadows. Second nature, he thought, watching the progress of the approaching figure. Came of many years of staying alive among wild men in wild country. You came to sense trouble instinctively, like an itch you knew was not for being ignored.

Doc Marley was in trouble. He had that look, even in this light. It was there in his walk, the way his body moved, but mostly in his face and the eyes that darted and swivelled in his head as if in a fever. And his walk was a dozen steps too hurried for a man of his age.

So what had disturbed him this bad at this hour to prompt this reaction, wondered Eli? Something to do with Grace Keene? Had her condition worsened? But if that were the case, why head for the sheriff's office? Scant sense to be raised there.

Eli glanced to left and right, scanning the street for any sign of Will Petty. No saying where he had holed-up after the shooting at the livery. Well, the fellow would surface again when he was good and ready, he guessed. Seemed to be his way. Meantime, there was Doc, the look in his eyes and that walk.

'Doc!' hissed Eli, craning from the shadows as the man drew level. 'It's me, Eli. You ain't lookin' so good. Anythin' I can do? Miss Keene makin' progress?'

Doc had hesitated, his steps slowed, head turned, but he had not stopped.

Eli kept pace, still hugging the shadows. 'Hey, Doc, what's the hurry?' he asked. 'You want some help?'

'That fancy-coated saloon-keeper out of Miriam is holdin' Miss Keene hostage at my place. And he figures you and Will brought her in,' muttered Doc from the corner of his mouth, his steps at the same even pace. 'There's a bank raid planned. They're after the gold. Porter and Crabbe are in on it. Find Will. Do what you can. The rat back there is watchin'. If I stop, he'll kill the woman. You got it?'

'Got it,' said Eli, easing deeper into the shadows as Doc drew ahead of him and stepped into the lantern glow at the sheriff's office. 'Hell,' he murmured to himself. 'Just that – just hell!'

It was a full ten minutes before Eli found Will sharing a pot of fresh coffee with Bart Parnham in the shadowy silence of the livery forge. They listened almost without blinking as he told of his brief meeting with Doc.

'Sonsof-goddamn-bitches,' stormed Bart, placing his steaming mug on the bench at his side. 'What in hell's name we goin' to do about that? If Crabbe's sided along of Porter, we ain't got no law. And there ain't time to go speedin' up the marshal's arrival – that gold shipment is due to be moved out in a couple of days.' He reached absently for a stained, sooty rag to wipe his sweat-damp hands. 'Dare we try gettin' Miss Keene out of Doc's place? One helluva risk with her in the condition she is.'

'I seen a whole crowd of townsmen in the saloon – and they weren't on no social gatherin',' said Eli. 'I'd figure for their mood bein' a mite tetchy. Winter may have reckoned for Will here bein' the loose gun about town, but the men ain't for knowin', leastways not yet.'

'But they're on the move in search of me by the look of it,' murmured Will, from the shadows at the forge's open front. 'See for yourselves.'

The three men watched without a word between them as the first of the torches flared in the hands of the gathering crowd at the saloon.

'Every home, every business, every barrel and crate,' called a voice above the murmurings of the others. 'No place gets overlooked. And when we find him, you just remember we're the law in this town and we got a right to make it safe against gunslingers.'

Bart swallowed on a dry, dusty throat and twisted the rag to a ball. Will's eyes narrowed to piercing lights. Eli pushed at his hat and spat.

'I hope you're figurin' for all this, Will Petty,' he murmured, as the townsmen headed for the far end of the main street.

TWENTY

Rope Porter paced the length of Doc Marley's dimly lit parlour, reached the window, stared thoughtfully into the street for a moment, then grunted as he swung round. 'Can she be moved?' he rasped, his gaze flashing like a light across Doc's face.

'Hell, no,' croaked Doc, adjusting his spectacles. 'She'd be lucky to make it to the top of the street there. I'm tellin' you, fella, Grace Keene is in no fit state —'

'Top of the street will be far enough when the time comes,' grinned Porter. 'What you reckon, Blake? You followin' my thinkin'?'

The saloon owner picked at a fleck of dirt on the lapel of his coat. 'Perfectly,' he said, flicking the speck into space. 'As a hostage, she'll be worth her weight in gold, so to speak.' He smiled arrogantly. 'Which was, of course, my original thinkin'.'

Otis Crabbe shifted his stance uncomfortably. 'Yeah, well, you can hold up there, pair of you. Before you get carried away, you'd best set your minds to reckonin' how I'm goin' to contain them townsmen out there. Seems to me they might be takin' matters into their own hands.' He pointed to the partially draped window. 'Take a look. See for yourselves.'

'I've looked. I've seen,' growled Porter. 'There's no problem. Nothin' we can't handle.'

'We?' frowned Crabbe. '*We* can't handle? And just what the hell are you proposin' now?'

'Whatever, you ain't goin' to get away with it,' huffed Doc. 'Tell yuh that for nothin'.'

'You ain't bein' consulted,' snapped Porter. 'Stick with the doctorin', all right?'

Doc mouthed a curse and thrust his spectacles defiantly to the bridge of his nose.

'Now here's what we do,' continued Porter, glancing quickly to the window again. 'We're goin' to put this night to good use; save ourselves a whole wagon of effort tomorrow. We're goin' to take up residence in the bank – all of us, includin' the woman.'

'We're goin' to what?' spluttered Crabbe. 'You must be mad! How in the name of fryin' rattlers we goin' to do that?'

'Crazy,' murmured Doc.

'Spend the night there, with the woman as hostage until sun-up, help ourselves to the gold, then we simply pull out,' mused Porter.

Doc gulped and stared wide-eyed. Crabbe pushed his hat clear of his sweating brow.

Porter turned back to the window. 'Next move is for you to get out there, Sheriff, and hold them townsmen well clear of the bank,' he ordered brusquely. 'You'll think of a way. Meantime, Doc here will get the woman on her feet and ready to move. We'll then make our way to the rear of the bank and be there by the time you, Otis, have persuaded that bank manager fella to accompany you to his office for a check on the security arrangements in view of the town unrest. And make sure the rat brings his keys – all of them!' Porter turned again, his grin wet and twitchy. 'We're goin' to need all the guns we can lay our hands on – just in case – and a guarantee of horses. But the sheriff here will see to all that, I'm sure.'

'Won't work,' growled Doc. 'Not in a million years.'

'One more moanin' peep out of you, old man, and you won't never be workin' again in any capacity,' threatened Porter. 'I lost two good partners over this and I ain't for losin' nothin' more.'

'Sure you have,' smirked Doc, 'and you still don't know who killed 'em do you? Too right you don't. Tell you some-thin', though, he's still out there and, by my reckonin', still waitin'.'

The sweat on Crabbe's brow began to gleam. Winter dismissed the flecks of dirt and glanced at the door to the bedroom. Porter turned back to the window.

'That's right, Mr Porter, you just keep watchin',' smiled Doc.

Will Petty waited in the shadows for the glow of the townsmen's flares to pass before he tapped the butt of his holstered Colt and slid away into the depths of the night.

He moved quickly, silently, dodging with ease between the scatterings of clutter at the rear of the main-street buildings, pausing only to watch the progress of the flares and listen to the men's shouted orders among themselves.

He would reach Doc Marley's place well ahead of the search party, have time to assess the situation and make a decision on the chances of snatching Grace Keene free without the risk of the lead flying high and wild.

If he could leave her safe at the livery with Bart Parnham and Eli, he could attend to his other business with a clear mind. And he was not for missing a second of that, he thought, on a lick of his lips.

He slid on, conscious for a fleeting moment of the bank in a seemingly slumbering darkness, save for the dim flicker of the night guard's single lantern in a back room. Now, as he left the crowded rear of the neighbouring Kearney Mercantile, he had the shape and bulk of Doc's home clear in his sight.

A low light burned in the parlour; nothing in any of the bedrooms or across the porch, and only Doc's mount hitched at the rail. A peaceful setting that might have graced any night in a thriving town, thought Will, still hugging the deep shadows as he crept closer.

But what you saw was not always what you got.

He had come to the edge of the thickest of the shadows and paused to rate his chances of crossing to the porch, when a glow of light sprang into life beneath the back door. Will eased away, waited, concentrated his gaze on the door, listened for sounds but caught no more than the voices of the approaching band of townsmen.

The door creaked open. Doc Marley glanced hurriedly left to right, to the left again, straight ahead for a moment, then closed the door and doused the light.

Will grunted quietly to himself. What had Doc been looking for or expecting to see, he wondered? Was he alone in the house, or were Porter and Winter with him? And just where was the sheriff?

'Hold it there, boys,' called Crabbe as if in answer to Will's pondering as the sheriff joined the townsmen some distance away. 'Time you all took a rest, caught up on some sleep, eh? I can tell you for a fact there ain't nothin' to be found this end of town. Had a close look myself. So what say you have a night cap? Have it on me. How's that strike yuh?'

'Strikes me well enough!' piped a man in the crowd. 'Me too,' echoed another.

The gathering murmured its agreement and began to shuffle away towards the main street and the saloon.

'You've done a good job here, boys,' said Crabbe, ushering the men along. 'Grateful to you. What I like to see. Town spirit, eh? Yeah, town spirit. . . .' The voices faded, the night silence closed in.

And Doc Marley's back door opened again.

Will's fingers flexed anxiously, danced on the butt of his Colt, then stiffened with the rest of his body as he watched the figures slip like dark moths to the porch.

Rope Porter was the first to appear, wait a moment, watch, listen, his eyes white as lights on the darkness before glancing back to gesture for the others to follow.

The slow, shuffling shape of Grace Keene, her steps uncertain, head lowered, body wrapped in the folds of a blanket, followed under Doc's gentle guidance. She hesitated twice, almost as if to raise her head and gaze round her, only to be urged on under Porter's impatient gestures.

Blake Winter, straightening the drape of his coat as he emerged from the back room, was the last to appear, closing the door softly behind him.

Porter halted the party, gestured for maximum silence, stared for a moment at the woman, then stepped clear of the porch and into the night, his steady steps heading back towards the town.

Will cleared a thin line of sweat from his top lip and moved through the shadows, his thoughts racing with the likely scheming in Rope Porter's mind. He was holding Grace Keene hostage, that much was plain; the ace card in an unknown pack. He had lost his partners, but still had the value of Crabbe at his side, and was probably suffering the partnership of Blake Winter – both likely to die at his hand once he had secured the gold.

So what would be his next move?

Will quickened his step to draw level with and then ahead of the party. They continued to move slowly, the steps measured, but still in a direct line. To where? Will's eyes narrowed on the shadowy bulks of surrounding shapes: the black backs of the buildings, the blind, unwelcoming doors and windows, discarded clutter, no lights. . . . Save for one.

The duty guard's lantern at the bank!

'Damnit, yes!' hissed Will under his breath. Rope Porter and his party were moving into the bank.

Will watched as Porter began to turn from the direct line and close on the single light. Two bits to a slice of bad pie Crabbe had already taken care of the guard in some way and the door Porter was approaching would be open.

'Hell!' cursed Will again, his weight slipping to one foot

as his teeth gritted and his body tensed. But it was the shift of his stance, the jolt of his boot against an empty crate, that cracked the night silence like a shot.

Porter swung round, his glare suddenly wild, one hand brushing Doc and the woman to the back of him, the other filling instantly with the gleaming bulk of his Colt.

Winter had similarly drawn a fancy-handled gun from his holster and swung round, crouching low, in the direction of the noise.

'Who the hell's there?' hissed Porter, his glare burning into the darkness. 'Go see,' he gestured to Winter. 'We ain't for attractin' an audience.'

The saloon keeper hesitated, glanced at Porter, then at Doc and the cowering woman.

'Do it,' insisted Porter, thrusting his Colt into space.

Winter squirmed his shoulders, worked his fingers to a firmer grip on his weapon and eased slowly, carefully forward, his steps as soft as an animal's stalking its supper.

'And if you see anythin' out there, shoot it,' spat Porter, bundling Doc and Grace Keene into the deeper shadows before narrowing his gaze on the dim light in the window at the bank. 'Hurry it along, f'Cris'sake,' he clipped impatiently.

Will screwed his face in the effort of avoiding more noise as he struggled to find his balance, at the same time watching Winter creeping steadily forward. He reached for the side of a crate, flattened his hand on its top and pushed himself back from a half crouching position, only to feel the crate shift and hear it groan.

Winter spun on his heel, the gun blazing at no more than sound. Three shots, fast and levelled over the short distance, the aim blind but close enough for the second shot to burn through the flesh at Will's shoulder, twist him back to the crate and crash him to the ground with a thud.

He lay perfectly still, the blood coursing freely from the wound to the dirt, his eyes wide open, waiting, watching for the looming bulk of Blake Winter.

'Leave it,' shouted Porter from the shadows. 'Them shots'll bring half the town squirmin' round us. Let's go!'

Winter stared into the darkness for a moment as if expecting it to crack, swallowed tightly and turned away.

Will heaved a long sigh and flattened his fingers in his own blood.

TWENTY-ONE

'Just hold yourself still there, will yuh? Bad enough tryin' to do this without a doc. No point in you makin' it worse, Will Petty. Hell!' Eli smacked his lips, fixed the bandage into place and stood back to assess his efforts. 'Though I say it m'self, that ain't half bad for a plain man. Not bad at all.' He thrust his hands into the bowl of water on the table at his side. 'Ain't guaranteein' as how you'll live, o'course – I ain't that good – but you're sure as hell goin' to have an easy time from here on. No more escapadin' around for you, fella. Nossir!'

The gathering of townsmen in the Gold Rush saloon glanced nervously at the wounded man – still pondering who and what he was – then went back to their anxious patrolling of the windows and batwings.

'Quiet enough out there, now,' murmured a lean fellow, squinting through a smeared pane.

'Goin' to be 'til they're good and ready to make their next move, ain't it?' said a stouter man at the batwings.

'And we all know what that's goin' to be,' added his partner. He blew a thick cloud of angry smoke from a newly lit cheroot. 'Just knew we should never have trusted that two-bit sheriff,' he added tautly. 'Knew it. Should've ousted him months back.'

'Too late for that now,' said Bart Parnham from his seat at a corner table. 'We've all seen what's happened; we all know what Crabbe, Porter and that dandy saloon keeper are plannin'. Damnit, they've even got the bank's manager holed-up with 'em! And there ain't no doubtin' to what they're plannin' for Grace Keene, though I wouldn't be for givin' Doc Marley a deal of a future.'

Bart came to his feet, walked the length of the bar to the batwings and stared into the night. 'And we can only wait,' he murmured.

'Mebbe we could round up all them as is willin' and storm the bank,' offered the lean man, blinking rapidly. 'Hit the place like a plains' wind.'

'Sure,' said Bart to the night, 'and spend the next day mopping up the blood and settin' out the dead bodies.' He turned back to the bar. 'You volunteerin'?'

'Well —' began the man, only to lose his way on a suddenly croaking voice.

'Only fools would get to thinkin' along them lines,' grunted Eli. 'Porter and the scum along of him would pick us off like flies.'

'But if we ain't for hittin' the place – and I sure as hell can't see many steppin' forward for the chance – what are we supposed to do?' asked a man at the bar. 'Do we send for help? Mebbe we should raise the miners out at Silvertown. Damnit, it's their gold!'

'We've got that covered already,' said Bart. 'Col Simmonds left for Silvertown an hour back. The miners'll get here, sure enough, but not in time. Porter will make his break at first light with the woman as his cover. Meantime, he's got all night to open up the safes and start packin'!'

'Hold it there,' called a fellow watching from a window fronting the street, 'somebody at the bank is movin'.' He squinted into the darkness as the others gathered at his shoulder and jostled at the batwings. 'Ain't that Doc Marley?' he asked, tightening his squint.

'That's Doc,' said the stout man.

'And that glint of a gun at his back is certain as sun-up in Porter's hand,' clipped Bart.

The men fell silent, tense and concentrated as they watched Doc shuffle to the edge of the deeper shadows on the boardwalk at the bank, and seemed hardly to breathe as his voice cracked across the night.

'You fellas out there can see for yourselves well enough what the situation is here.' He paused a moment, glancing down the street. The prod of a gun barrel in his back prompted him to continue. 'I'm to tell you that Miss Keene is alive, but that any move against the bank and the fellas holdin' it will result in the lady. . . . Guess you understand what I'm sayin'.' Doc paused again. 'And that's it for now. Just don't make any move – please, for the woman's sake.'

Doc was pulled back to the darkness; a door slammed; somewhere a dog howled balefully.

'So that's that,' grunted Bart. 'Plain enough, ain't it? Couldn't have made it any clearer.'

Eli pulled angrily at the brim of his hat and hitched his pants with a flourish. 'Sonsof-goddamn-bitches,' he cursed, pushing his way from the jostle at the 'wings.

'What you reckon, Will? How in hell are we —'

But the chair where the wounded man had been seated was empty.

'Goddamnit if that fella don't try a man to madness!' fumed Eli, snatching his hat from his head as his gaze followed the trail of blood spots to the saloon's back door.

Doc Marley took Grace Keene's hand and gave it a reassuring squeeze. 'And that, ma'am, sparin' the details, is about the sum total of it,' he murmured, glancing quickly over the woman's shoulder to the group of men gathered in the yellow glow of a lantern at the far end of the bank's main office. 'T'ain't a pretty picture, and I'm sure as hell sorry you're involved like you are. Bein' dragged out there just now and forced to say what I did don't sit easy neither.'

'I understand, Doc,' said Grace hoarsely, a smile flickering at her cracked lips. 'You don't have to spell it out any clearer than you have. I just regret being as ill as I've have been, but I'm feeling a whole lot better now.'

'Good to hear it, but you just go easy. You're weak and this situation ain't goin' to be one bit of a help.'

'The question is, what are we going to do? We can't just wait, can we?'

Doc sighed. 'You got any better ideas, ma'am? Too damned obvious what them scum there are plannin': way they see it, while ever they've got you, they're holdin' all the cards.'

Grace turned and shivered at the sound of the movements behind her.

Eli was still cursing as he stumbled through the saloon's

back door to the night and the eerie emptiness of an uncertain town.

'Goddamnit,' he moaned, bending low to squint for a continuation of the trail of blood spots, 'what in the name of sanity you got in mind now, Will Petty?' He grunted quietly as he bent lower. 'You just don't never get to listenin' to any good advice, do you? Oh, no, not you! Just go boundin' ahead as if there ain't no t'day and precious little prospect of t'morrow. . . .'

'There, ahead of you,' said Bart Parnham, appearing at the old man's side. 'He's still losin' blood, sure enough, and looks to be headin' for my place. Now what in hell does he want with a horse at this time of night in his condition? He plannin' on ridin' out or somethin'?'

'Not him, not Will Petty,' grunted Eli, settling his floppy hat. 'Not while Rope Porter's still alive and holdin' Grace Keene. He won't be for pullin' out of that business, whatever his condition.'

'Then we'd best go see what he finds so intriguin' at the livery,' said Bart, laying an arm across Eli's shoulders.

They slid away, staying low and moving fast through the flotsam and clutter, and were lost to the deeper darkness like bats on the wing.

They met no one, saw no one, heard nothing save the occasional raised voice at the saloon and were into the silent, brooding mass of shadows at the deserted livery in what seemed only seconds.

Bart halted them as they approached the stabling. 'Your friend's here,' he whispered, 'far side of the straw barn.'

Eli's eyes narrowed to dark slits. 'What in tarnation is he doin'?'

'Well, if I wasn't seein' it for myself,' began Bart, craning forward, 'I'd say he was loadin' up that old wagon of mine with just about anythin' that comes to hand and he can lift.'

'If he don't try a man. . . .' spluttered Eli, strutting ahead on long strides. 'And just what,' he seethed, as he drew closer to Will and the wagon, 'do you think you're doin' now, f'Cris'sake?'

Will turned, a half bale of straw perched in his arms. 'Figured you'd be here sooner or later.' He nodded at Bart and heaved the half bale into the buckboard. 'Lend a hand here, if you would.'

'Hold on,' said Bart, stepping closer. 'I don't recall bookin' no order for a loaded wagon to leave my livery, and I certainly wouldn't have reckoned for it pullin' out at this time of night, so mebbe you'd care to tell me, mister, just what in hell you're plannin' here?'

'Preparin' to attack the bank; stop them scumbags from liftin' a heap of gold and, if I get really lucky, givin' Miss Grace Keene some peaceful nights' sleep.'

'Oh, sure,' mocked Eli, 'and just everybody would know that an old, full-loaded wagon is just the thing to do it!'

Will threw a length of split planking aboard the wagon, winced at a stab of pain in his shoulder and tightened his expression to a grey unblinking mask. 'We ain't got a hope in hell of hittin' that bank all guns blazin' like we were on a drunken hoe-down. Grace Keene would be dead in seconds, twenty and mebbe more men along of her.'

'We know that well enough,' clipped Bart.

'So we've mebbe got to trust to some lucky chance comin' our way,' added Eli.

'No, we ain't,' snapped Will, his eyes gleaming. 'We make our chances. We take a fight to them, first hint of light.' He slapped a hand on the side of the wagon. 'And this, gentlemen, is how we're goin' to do it, assumin' Mr Parnham's permission for the use of the outfit. But we'll do it, anyhow.' He paused, his stare like flame on the men's faces. 'Time ain't exactly on our side, so shall we get to it?'

Bart simply blinked. Eli licked his lips and pulled his hat tight on his head.

TWENTY-TWO

'Don't worry, my dear, you will be well cared for – very well cared for. You have my word on it.' Blake Winter's smile was slow and easy, his gaze icily flat on Grace Keene's face.

'And your word, Blake, isn't worth a spit,' sneered Grace. 'It never was, and it sure as sun-up ain't now.' She shrugged her shoulders irritably. 'You're out of your depth here, you know that, don't you? Fast-shooting, hard-drinking bank raiders are not your company. You don't fit.'

She tossed her hair petulantly, smiled hurriedly at Doc and strolled slowly to the window overlooking the street. 'Be full light in an hour,' she murmured. 'Is that when you plan on riding out with the gold?'

'Keep that woman's mouth shut, will yuh?' growled Crabbe, from the depths of the bank's main office. 'She don't need to know. She's here for one purpose and one purpose only.' He glanced anxiously at the ashen-faced manager hovering at the two safes in the corner. 'Once we're clear of town, she's as worthless as the rest.'

The manager shuddered and swallowed noisily. 'I got a wife and family,' he began, swallowing again.

'Good for you,' chuckled Porter. 'That's what all men should have, eh, Winter? Nice little wife, nice little family. Mebbe you'll get to it when this is over. Wed that bar whore there. Give her a decent life.'

Grace flared, stiffened, but stayed silent. Doc flushed with anger.

Winter merely grinned. 'And I might at that,' he said. 'Yeah, I just might.'

'Let's get movin',' ordered Crabbe. 'All this talk's wastin' time. Get them safes open and start countin'.' He jangled a bunch of keys in his fingers. 'This way to the good times?'

Doc glanced at the clock on the wall, then at Grace who went back to counting the shadows in the empty street.

The townsmen, still uncertain of what to do, where to be – other than the bar of the saloon – had not moved through the long hours of night. They had kept watch on the bank from the batwings, the windows, and once, risking as they saw it their very necks, from the boardwalk.

'Types like Porter don't mess when there's gold in their sights,' an old man had remarked between generous measures of whiskey. 'I go back some and recall the time out Rockforth when that sonofabitch, Matt Kirks, hit the Borders Bank and took the manager's wife – *wife*, no less – as hostage against him ridin' free. Goddamnit, never did see such a change in a fella. Went stark-ravin' mad and left the woman pregnant. Yessir, did just that.'

'You ain't sayin' —' a serious-looking young man had begun.

'Old fella there ain't sayin' nothin',' the stout man had

snapped, 'save that we don't get booze-boosted and start figurin' we can take Porter in a hell-raisin' shoot-out. We can't. We wait.'

'We wait,' others had echoed, grateful to stay where they were and let the first light usher in whatever the fates had in store for Kearney.

And they did not have long to wait.

First hint of the events to come was given by Bart Parnham as the light cleared the eastern ranges.

'Now listen up, all of you,' Bart had urged, when he reached the bar through the back door. 'Fella you all know now as Will Petty, with that old-timer, Eli, along of him, has worked out a plan, a way to mebbe shift Porter and them vermin out of the bank, save the woman and the Silvertown gold.'

'Goin' to have to be one helluva plan,' said the stout man watching the street from the batwings.

'What's he got in mind?' asked a tired-eyed youth. 'We got enough guns among us to hold Fort Benham.'

'Yeah, well, that's just what we don't want,' said Bart. 'Flyin' lead is almost certain to lose us the woman and no sayin' how many innocent townsfolk. We ain't for creatin' a bloodbath.'

'So what's the fella plannin'?'

'He wants the street absolutely clear. Nobody on the sidewalks. Everybody indoors 'til he's through. But from the minute he makes his move, he wants the bank covered. A dozen guns ranged on it, steady, level, and silent. He'll shout the orders when the time comes.'

'All well and good,' nodded the stout man, 'but just

what is this move goin' to be, and when's he goin' to make it? I don't see how. . . .'

Bart tightened a hand on the 'wings and stared into the grey breaking light in the street as if listening to its creep. 'You're just about to,' he murmured. And then the sound began to roll across that dawn like something summoned from the darkest hills.

The grinding rumble of heavy wheels grew to a pitched moan, the creaking of timbers, pound of hoofs. A dust-cloud thickened and swirled at the far end of town beyond the livery, the faint light shafting through it in beams and shimmers.

The ground seemed to shake as if being punched from hidden depths; horses snorted, a whip cracked like gunshot, and a voice, lifting to frenzied shouts above the rolling roar, cut across the morning with its hell-fire curses.

The stout man's eyes widened through a haze of sudden sweating. 'I don't believe it,' he croaked.

'We've loaded up my old wagon with all the rubbish you can imagine,' said Bart, as the townsmen jostled to his shoulder at the 'wings. 'Will Petty and Eli figure on —'

'Goddamnit, I can see what they got in mind,' groaned a man from behind a stream of cigar smoke. 'They're goin' to . . . hell's alive . . . they're goin' to use the wagon to ram the bank!'

'And they'd better get shiftin',' croaked the stout man again. 'Porter and his rats ain't goin' to be for layin' out a welcome mat!'

'Get your guns levelled, boys,' ordered Bart. 'But keep 'em quiet. Let Will Petty do it his way.'

The wagon rolled and rumbled into the length of the street, Eli at the reins, Will straddling the back of one of the pair of wild-eyed horses straining to heave the loaded wagon.

'Go to it, m'beauties!' yelled Eli, swirling and cracking the whip high above his head. 'Go to it!' He glanced anxiously at Will, tightened his grip on the bunch of reins, cracked the whip again and rolled his balance to the swing and lurch of the wagon.

Will's hands were wet with a hot, slippery sweat where he gripped the tack, his legs numb in their strain to hold his weight to the heaving horse, his shoulder throbbing with poker-hot spasms of pain.

His eyes narrowed. The street seemed to close in, the buildings to tighten as if about to reach out to throttle him, but ahead were the lights of the saloon, the shadowy shapes of men, and beyond them on the opposite side the black brooding bulk of the bank.

And Rope Porter.

Will gritted his teeth, half turned to glance at Eli. 'You ready?' he shouted.

Eli cracked the whip and whooped at the top of his voice. 'You got it, Mr Petty! Good and ready whenever you are – and if I don't see you in Heaven, I'll sure as damnation see you in Hell!'

He whooped again, cracked the leather and rose on his bent, aged legs from the driver's seat to stand against the morning light like a spectre, dust swirling round him, wheels spinning beneath him.

Will waited only seconds, his fingers fumbling at his belt for the shape of his knife. His eyes narrowed again.

'Now!' he shouted.

The first morning light seemed to crack and splinter as Eli released another almighty whoop, tossed the reins into space and leapt like a cat from the wagon to the street, thudding painfully into the dirt with a curse and a long, throaty moan.

He rolled, spluttering dust and saliva, and scrambled to his knees in time to see Will make one last lunge with his knife at the loosely fixed tack to cut the snorting team free of the wagon.

'There she goes!' yelled Eli, staggering to his feet as Will made his own leap clear of the rolling mass before it began to slew, threatened to topple across the street, then slewed again, this time mounting the boardwalk fronting the bank.

The creaking, groaning wagon packed tight with the everyday flotsam of Bart Parnham's livery, crashed through the bank's windows and main door with a shuddering, splintering rush, shattering glass, splitting walls, the slewing wheels grinding over floorboards, the sheer weight and bulk of the mass reducing the once staid and formal bank interior to scattered slivers of wood and glass.

Eli kicked dirt, glanced quickly at Will, nodded and disappeared into the nearest alley leading to the rear of the bank.

'Somebody go round up that team and calm 'em,' shouted Will to the townsmen craning for a view from the saloon batwings. 'No shootin', not 'til we've secured the woman.' He swung round to the bank, his face and clothes dust and grime caked. 'Doc? Doc Marley – you there?'

A shot spat to kick dirt at Will's feet.

'I'll tell you who's here, yuh sonofabitch,' cursed

Crabbe clambering over the splintered timbers, his Colt drawn, blood trickling from a head wound. 'And I'll go one better and show you, damn it!'

He fired a wild, blind shot high over Will's head.

Will crouched low, his gun clear of its holster, his gaze tight and steady through the haze of dust. 'Throw down that piece, Sheriff,' he called. 'I ain't for takin' you out, but if that's the way of it —'

Crabbe's Colt spat again, the lead searing the air to within a fraction of Will's wounded shoulder. 'Go to hell, Will Petty,' he growled, levelling his gun for a third shot, his body balanced like a stranded insect on the heaped destruction. 'Sonofa. . . .'

But that was the last sound to leave Sheriff Otis Crabbe's lips. In the next moment, he had gulped, rolled his eyes at the speed of Will's blazing retort and sprawled face-down in the destruction like something thrown out to the trash.

Will blinked, cleared his eyes and swallowed. He half turned to the saloon where Bart Parnham and the townsmen had gathered. 'I'm goin' in,' he shouted. 'Cover me. Don't let nobody ride out. Shoot 'em if you have to.'

He crossed quickly to the dust-shrouded, shadowed remains of the bank, clambered over the mound of broken timbers and was blinking on the silent, light-filtered gloom of the once grand office when a gun-hammer clicked and he froze where he stood.

'I think you've come far enough, Mr Petty. So let's call it a day, shall we?'

TWENTY-THREE

Will hesitated, blinking again, his eyes working to make out the shape of Blake Winter balanced on a jumble of timbers in the shadows, his Colt gleaming firm and steady in his grip.

'Ain't you just been the busy one?' grinned the saloon-bar proprietor, his stare fixed and unblinking. 'I was beginnin' to think we might not make it, but let me assure you, in case you're wonderin', the gold is here. We have it.' He shrugged nonchalantly. 'Share out's gettin' bigger by the minute now that you've had the last word with Sheriff Crabbe out there.' The grin faded. 'You've had your say – very dramatically – and you've had your day.'

'Where's Miss Keene,' snapped Will, his eyes narrowing to probe the gloom beyond Winter.

'Ah, yes, the famous Miss Keene you've taken such an interest in. Bet you half wish now you never rode out of Miriam with her trail-hitched to you. Been some trouble, ain't she? And you with only killin' in mind – retribution, way I'm seein' it, fella. Should've guessed from how you handled that drunken scum back there in Miriam.

But no more. You've had your last killin', Mr Petty.'

Winter prodded the Colt to a new aim. 'We're wastin' my time here,' he quipped.

'Mine too,' said Will, grunting as he hooked his boot under a length of timber and hoisted it across Winter's gun hand.

The timber scraped across Winter's wrist. The Colt blazed, but the shot was high and wide. Winter cursed, tried desperately to steady his aim, glared at Will and made to lunge forward, only to stumble, miss his footing and begin to topple to his left.

'Damn you!' spat Winter, his arms spreading, the gun waving uselessly. His trigger-finger worked instinctively. Another shot burned into space but it was to be the last from the gleaming Colt as Will's gun spat once, twice, throwing Winter back to the deeper shadows where his body clattered into the splintered timbers and lay still, the dust settling like snow on the folds and pleats of his frock coat.

Will cleared a haze of sweat from his brow, gave the body no more than a cursory glance, and clambered on, over the broken structures, the scattered junk from Bart's livery, delving deeper into the bank to where he guessed the safes were located.

He halted, half crouching, eyes burning at the sound of a movement ahead of him. Where in hell was Porter, where were Grace and Doc Marley, and what of the bank manager the raiders had held hostage?

He had his answer to the fate of the manager in his next step over the clutter. He swallowed, sweated and cursed under his breath at the sight of the man's body, his throat

slashed, blood already congealing in thick, sticky smears –
and beyond the body, the bank safes, their doors swung
open, the dark interiors as empty as gaping mouths, the
night guard dead at their sides. He cursed again, stumbled
and fell to his knees, then froze at the sound of Doc
Marley's voice.

'Easy does it there, Will,' he croaked. 'Porter's waitin'
on yuh, and he's got Grace. Don't have to spell out what
he's got in mind, do I?'

Will strained to probe the shadows and gloom for
shapes. 'Where are you, Doc?' he grunted. 'Can't see a
darned thing back there.'

'You don't need to, mister,' crowed Porter on a deep
hawk, a long spit and a cackled laugh. 'I can tell you plain
enough what I got here: I got enough gold to keep me in
real nice style for the rest of my born days, and I got me a
real good-lookin' woman here to tend to my creature
comforts.'

He cackled again. 'Not bad, eh? Not bad at all. Now all
I need is horses, seein' as how your old-timer friend
sprawled at my feet here saw fit to scatter my hitched
mounts before I had the pleasure of layin' a gun barrel
across his skull.'

Damn your eyes, thought Will, wincing as he eased
forward on his knees. If anything happened to the old
fellow. . . .

'But seein' as how you're so resourceful,' continued
Porter, 'I want you to go get those horses for me. And right
now. If you don't, or try gettin' smart again, well. . . .'

'He ain't foolin' none, Will,' grunted Doc. 'He'll kill us,
cold-blooded as it comes.'

'Very wise, Doc,' sneered Porter. 'Yuh hear that, mister?'

'I hear,' said Will, wincing again as he eased on through the creaking timbers. 'Same as I heard you back there on the trail to Miriam. You remember that day, Porter? You remember me?'

'Oh, yes, I remember you well enough, Mr Petty. Doc here's been refreshin' my memory. Seems I should've finished the job at that dry-bed creek, eh? Made a bad mistake there. Still, I ain't complainin' none. You've been a real pain in the butt here in Kearney, and I ain't for bein' forgivin' over the shootin' of my partners. But, hell, I've got the gold, ain't I, and you've brought me the woman, so who's complainin'?' He hawked and spat. 'Just go get them horses. Right now!'

'Best do it, Will,' quaked Doc. 'Grace ain't lookin' good. Don't reckon for her takin' much more, and Eli's in sore need of attention.'

Will screwed his eyes for a moment at the pain in his shoulder, then gazed carefully ahead to the shadowy, dust-laden gloom where the morning light was filtered through thin pale beams. He waited, listening, picturing the men in the saloon, recalling the trail into Miriam, the wagon, the voices and sneering faces of the bushwhackers, cut of the knife-edge creek rocks on his naked body. . . .

'We ain't got all day,' called Porter.

'F'Cris'sake, Will —' groaned Doc.

But even as Doc's voice grated over his parched throat and his gaze flashed fearfully to Grace Keene held in a locked grip across Porter's body, Eli unconscious and bleeding at their feet, he was aware of a shadow building on the faint light.

He watched as the shape grew, darker, taller, the bulk seeming to breathe through the silence. 'Will. . . .' he mouthed, aware then of Porter's eyes narrowing, his grip on the woman tightening, the barrel of his gun cold and gleaming at her neck.

'Hell,' he mouthed again, and then felt his mouth drop open as Will Petty straddled the mound of broken, splintered timbers, his Colt levelled in a thrusting aim at Porter.

Neither man spoke; they simply stared, eyes probing into a past that swam and spun through a crowd of images for Will of a day, a time and place, faces and voices that had never ended or been silenced.

'You ease that trigger-finger so much as a whisker the wrong way, mister, and the woman's dead,' growled Porter.

Will did not move, seemed not to blink, only to stare through the grey light as if not seeing Grace and the fear in her own gaze.

'One wrong move, that's all it'll take,' warned Porter again. 'Now why don't you be a sensible fella and go get them horses?' He grinned. 'See these bags of gold at my feet here? Well, what say we share 'em, eh? Plenty to go round. In fact —'

Doc kicked angrily at a length of broken timber, and cursed. 'Of all the sonsof-goddamn-bitches. . . .'

But it was the clatter of the timber, the snap of a voice that broke Porter's attention, relaxed his grip on Grace and gave her the split second she needed to squirm from the locking arm and put the gunslinger off his balance.

Doc reached to grab Grace's hand; Porter's hold ripped

her shirt, the momentum swinging his gun hand from its aim.

And it was then that Will Petty's Colt spat its vengeance.

The shots came fast and with deadly accuracy throwing Porter back across the rubble of timber, shards of broken glass, dust and dirt. He growled only once, widened his eyes to fierce, burning moons and was finally still with an arm outstretched, the fingers of the hand frozen in a clawing reach for a bag of gold.

Will was sometime before his face relaxed, his gaze softened and he blinked on the glow of the full morning light.

'Ain't no good reason why an outfit sound as this shouldn't take us as far as we've a mind to go – clear through to California if you've a hankerin'. What you reckon, Miss Keene, you got a heart for California?'

Eli cracked the reins to the easy paced team, rolled to the pitch of the wagon and winked mischievously at the woman seated next to him.

Grace smiled and tossed her hair. 'Is it far?' she asked, without appearing to notice the sudden drawing level of the outrider.

'Well, now,' mused Eli, pushing at his floppy hat, 'that depends. Could be just about any distance you so choose, but when the bank back there at Kearney and the miners out Silvertown show their gratitude for what we've saved 'em, with the gift of an outfit and provisions like this, well, I reckon you could make California real easy. Yessir, I do at that.'

Grace glanced quickly at the rider, then settled her gaze on the trail again. 'Some send-off they gave us at Kearney.

Whole town was beginning to look brighter and cleaner.'
She stifled a brief shiver. 'And with that marshal taking
charge, and Doc and Bart Parnham watchin' over things,
could be they've got a whole new future coming up there.'

'But not for you, eh, ma'am?' said Eli.

'I think not, Mr Cornpaw. No, my days of towns and
bars, gamblers, fast-talkers, gunslingers and double-deal-
ers are over. After Miriam and Kearney, I figure for the
quieter life. A homestead some place. Mebbe out
California way. Who knows?' She glanced quickly again at
the rider.

'Now that's one hell of a decent ambition, ma'am, and
I got a gut feelin' you'll make it.'

'*We'll* make it, Mr Cornpaw. You come with the outfit,
surely?'

Eli smacked his lips. 'Well, now, mebbe Mr Petty might
have somethin' to say about that. We go back some; a long
way in what seems now a long time. I wouldn't want to be
doin' nothin' he didn't go along with. And, damnit, somebody's gotta keep a watch on him! Ain't that so, Will?'

The rider reined close, his hands easy, gaze fresh and
watchful. 'We head due west, Mr Cornpaw. Had that in
mind a long ways back, before. . . . Yeah, well, what's past
is past, done and finished.' He shrugged his shoulder.
'Wound here should be mended by the time we get there
and you, ma'am, should be feelin' a whole sight better.
You're welcome to travel as far as we go. My pleasure.'

'Mine, too, Mr Petty,' smiled Grace.

Eli cracked the reins, and winked – this time at the
fellow he had found by chance in a dead man's creek.